"YOU BASTARD," BREATHED DALTON.

Rising, he swept the Whitney from his belt, his eyes blazing with a murderous rage.

The soldier took another step back as he fired, jarring his gun arm against the wall of the hotel, and the bullet made an ugly, cracking sound as it missed Dalton by scant inches. Dalton didn't even flinch. He aimed the Whitney and squeezed the trigger. He had been under fire too many times to be unnerved by the experience. The bullet made a neat, blue hole in the soldier's forehead, then blew the back of his skull off, splattering blood and brains all over the wall. The soldier's corpse hit the boardwalk so hard it bounced.

Dalton whirled at the sound of footsteps. Another soldier appeared in the hotel doorway. He looked at Margaret, at the dead bluecoat, then at Dalton—and his eyes got wide as a prospector's pan. He threw his hands out in front of him, as though trying to fend Dalton off.

"Don't shoot!" he shrieked, his voice cracking. "I'm not—"

The Whitney spoke, and the bullet struck the soldier squarely in the chest, and he sprawled backwards on the threadbare carpet covering the lobby floor. His heels beat a quick tattoo and then he was gone.

Dalton knew what the man had been trying to say—that he wasn't armed.

GRAY WARRIOR

HANK EDWARDS

HarperPaperbacks
A Division of HarperCollinsPublishers

HarperPaperbacks   *A Division of* HarperCollins*Publishers*
10 East 53rd Street, New York, N.Y. 10022

Copyright © 1995 by Jason Manning
All rights reserved. No part of this book may be used or reproduced in any manner whatsoever without written permission of the publisher, except in the case of brief quotations embodied in critical articles and reviews. For information address HarperCollins*Publishers,*
10 East 53rd Street, New York, N.Y. 10022.

Cover illustration by Tony Gabrielle

First printing: October 1995

Printed in the United States of America

HarperPaperbacks and colophon are trademarks of HarperCollins*Publishers*

❖ 10 9 8 7 6 5 4 3 2 1

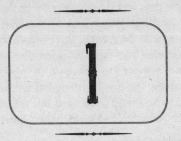

1865

Margaret Talcott stepped out onto the veranda, wearily sweeping a stray tendril of chestnut-brown hair from her eyes. She was an attractive young woman of twenty, slender and full of grace, but she did not feel at all attractive anymore. In the old days, before the war—days so vague in her memory that they seemed more like a dream than reality—she had been the belle of many a ball, and her appearance had been of very great and continuous importance to her. Today, though, her face and arms and dress were smudged with dirt and blood, and she was perspiring. It was a warm, muggy afternoon—this April the days had been unseasonably hot while the nights remained cool. But she had ceased to care about what she looked like. Why should she care what she looked like when the whole world was coming to an end.

She had been inside for hours, boiling water and making bandages and cooking food and tending to six wounded Confederate soldiers, and she was tired—so tired that the very marrow in her bones hurt. All she wanted was a moment's respite, and had come out onto the veranda for a breath of fresh air and to escape the misery and despair and defeat she saw in the eyes of the soldiers she and her father and Lucius were trying to help. But there was no escape. In the distance she could hear what sounded like faint thunder. She knew it to be cannons. And yonder, to the east, a ribbon of black smoke rose above the line of trees that marked the edge of what used to be a field of tobacco but was now an ugly expanse of churned-up red mud baked hard by today's sun.

There were two more soldiers on the veranda, and their eyes resembled those of the six inside. An old man and a young one. The latter's head was wrapped in a bloody bandage. The old man was barefoot, and his feet were swollen and discolored.

The old man touched the brim of his slouch hat.

"Beg pardon, miss. We didn't mean to intrude. But the boy here needed rest, and the shade of this here porch was right invitin'."

"What regiment are you with?"

"Fifth Virginia Volunteers. But I don't rightly know where the Fifth Virginia is, or even if it still exists, to tell the truth. Them bluebellies hit us day before yesterday. Hit us hard. Been separated from the regiment ever since, me and this boy here."

Margaret stepped closer. The young man sat beside the oldtimer, bent forward and rocking slowly. He seemed completely unaware of his surroundings. Bloodshot eyes stared blankly at the weathered planking of the veranda's floor.

"What's the matter with him?"

"Yankee artillery, ma'am. The regiment was dug in in some woods, waitin' for them Billy Yanks to charge right into us. We would've given 'em what for if they had, just like we done at Sharpsburg and Fredericksburg. But they didn't come. Nossir, they didn't. Didn't have to. Must've been a hunnerd big guns. Ain't nothin' left of them woods but a pile of burnt sticks. They just kept poundin' us until the trees they caught on fire. We finally broke and run. What was left of us. As I recollect, that was the first and only time the Fifth Virginia run. A lot of the wounded got caught in the fire. I can still hear 'em screaming." The old-timer looked away, blinked three times rapidly, and then shook his head like a man who is trying to clear the cobwebs. "I caint seem to get that screamin' out of my ears. I grabbed holt of this feller and pulled him out. Don't even know his name. He won't tell me. Ain't said a word in two days. It's like he's in another world."

"It's shock," said Margaret. The boy looked young, maybe seventeen, eighteen at the oldest, and he reminded her of her younger brother, and the memory pulled painfully at her heart. Robert had been eighteen when he'd gone off to war. She vaguely remembered that day, all bright and happy and full of pride and hope. Robert had gone off to fight for a glorious cause and died a miserable death at a place called Gettysburg in a charge that some now said had broken the back of the Confederacy and doomed it to the defeat it was suffering now.

"We don't want to be no bother, ma'am," said the old-timer. "If you had a cup of water to spare for the boy, though, I'd be obliged. Me, I don't need none."

"Don't be silly. You'll both have water. Lucius! Lucius, come out here at once."

An elderly black man, white-haired and bent-backed, shuffled out of the house.

"Lucius, would you please bring these men some water?"

"Yessum. Right away."

Margaret turned back to the old soldier. "Are you hungry? I'm afraid we don't have much. Some bread and . . . some meat."

"We don't want to take your food, no, ma'am. Just some shade and a little water and we'll be good as new."

Lucius returned with a bucket of water, which he set down between the two men. Using the ladle, he offered some to the oldtimer. The oldtimer tried to get the boy to drink first. But the boy wouldn't drink. The oldtimer kept trying. He was bound and determined that the boy would drink before he did.

Margaret's father emerged from the house looking very grim.

"What is it, Father?" she asked.

"One of those poor boys just died," said Talcott, with a gusty sigh. "Lucius, we will have to dig another grave."

"Yessuh. Right away."

Talcott bleakly scanned the reddish-brown ruined fields and the green line of trees in the distance as he listened to the cannon.

"They're getting closer, Maggie. My God, I can't believe the Yankees have taken Richmond. Why in heaven's name doesn't Lee turn and fight?"

"Beg pardon," said the oldtimer, "but Marsh Robert he ain't got much of an army left to fight with no more. We ain't got no artillery to speak of, and the cavalry ... well, there ain't much left of the cavalry either. Their horses are plumb wore out. Rest of us, we ain't got no shoes, nor food, nor ammunition. Ask me, there's just too durn many of them Billy Yanks. Back at Spotsylvania and Cold Harbour and in the Wilderness we mowed 'em down by the hunnerds, but they just kept coming. That feller Grant, he's like a bulldog, he is. Latches onto you and plumb won't let go till you're just tired out trying to kick him off."

Talcott glowered at the old soldier. Ordinarily, he was not one to tolerate defeatist talk—of which there had been a lot lately—and Margaret was afraid he was going to rebuke the old soldier, which in her opinion would be to scale ingratitude to its pinnacle. These brave men had struggled against mighty odds. Odds that were turning out to be impossible. They had fought and suffered and died for what they believed in, and now there was precious little fight left in them. Margaret was pragmatic enough to accept the inevitable; the Confederacy was doomed. But her father refused to believe that his only son had given his life for nothing. That was just the way he was made. It had taken him all of a year to accept the fact that Margaret's mother was dead. Personally, Margaret was in a way relieved that the war was ending. Saddened, yes, and apprehensive about what the future held in store for a vanquished people, but relieved because at least the killing would stop soon.

Before Talcott could speak, Lucius pointed down the road.

"Mo' soldiers," he said.

They turned to see the ragged column of Rebel infantry shuffling out of the trees into the hard yellow sunlight, and even at this distance, almost a half-mile, Margaret could somehow feel their exhaustion and pain.

It was easy to tell that the men slogging along the road towards the Talcott house were Confederates. There was no marching in step, no drum beating martial time, no straight and orderly ranks, no bayonets flashing in the sunlight or flags flapping in the breeze. There were no uniforms to speak of—these men wore some butternut-gray wool, but linsey-woolsey and other material as well. Anything they could get their hands on. Some wore forage caps on their heads, others slouch hats, and some were bareheaded. And even the officer in front was afoot. There weren't many of them, either. Margaret thought they numbered about thirty.

When they were near the house the officer leading this

pack of dark, ragged, fierce scarecrows turned and barked a hoarse order to fall out. The men sank to the ground. They had been pushed to the limits of endurance and beyond, and suddenly Margaret experienced a flood of tremendous pride in these sons of the South who had gone to hell and back for their homeland. Their faces were full of dirt and courage. They were a very small fragment of what was called the Army of Northern Virginia, an army which was disintegrating as it raced westward down these dusty roads, harried by a relentless foe, trying to escape before the jaws of the trap closed on them, but an army which in better and more glorious times had accomplished truly remarkable martial feats, always outnumbered and out-supplied, so that it had become a legend in its own time.

The officer stepped over the gate in the once-white picket fence which separated the road from the sassafras-shaded yard of the Talcott house. The post into which the gate's hinges had been nailed was splintered—only one of a thousand repairs which had been left undone around the place—and the officer had noticed this and decided not to risk doing further damage. He came up the weed-overgrown gravel walk and saluted Margaret's father.

Talcott nodded sternly. "Welcome, Captain. My name is Talcott. This is my daughter, Margaret. What news?"

The captain did not respond immediately. He swept the veranda and everyone on it with eyes that in a glance could know everything there was to know about a person—eyes that could see in the old soldier and the young two men whose war was over, that could glance at Lucius and know he was the faithful retainer, the only slave among many who had once worked this plantation whose devotion had prevented him from running away, that could tell that Talcott was a diehard Confederate whose pride blinded him to the cold, hard truth of this particular April in war-torn Virginia. And then those eyes lighted on Margaret, and she felt a peculiar, warm rush.

He was handsome in a rugged way, she thought, tall and broad in the shoulders, a lean, strong frame forged in the crucible of four years of campaigning. His hair and beard were jet black, and the eyes were so dark she thought at first they were black too, but then realized they were in fact a deep, almost violet, blue. In the captain's face Margaret saw something she had not seen in the face of any other Confederate warrior for days. No despair, but rather an indomitable will to live, and not just to live, but to prevail.

"Captain Jack Dalton, sir, at your service," said the officer, in an unhurried drawl. Not Virginian, thought Margaret, thoroughly intrigued. This man was from the Deep South. He touched the brim of his hat. "A pleasure, ma'am. Thirty-second Alabama. Part of the Army's rear guard, under the command of General Gordon."

"What's the meaning of that firing back to the east?"

Dalton glanced east, back down the road to the line of pine trees, and he gazed blankly in that direction for almost a full minute, as though he were retracing in his mind's eye the long march he and his men had endured to reach this house, over and around hills, plunging into cold, fast-running creeks, across tilting, ruined fields, through difficult, brush-choked ravines and thickets of wild plums and azaleas in bloom.

"A big fight at Sayler's Creek," he said, finally. "The enemy has driven a wedge between the tail of Longstreet's corps and Anderson's. We were ordered to follow the supply train, to save the headquarters' wagons, but the Yank artillery poured it on us, and the train had to be abandoned, what was left of it. I'm afraid they have cut us to pieces."

"Is there no hope?" cried Talcott.

Dalton fixed that dark gaze on him. "The men and horses—what few horses that are left—are completely worn down by fatigue and hunger. My company has had only a handful of parched corn a day per man in the last four days. Thousands are leaving their regiments now. Wandering in every direction, foraging for food. Most of them have thrown down their weapons."

"Good God."

"But you ask if there is hope? I say there is always hope. Some of us are still trying to reach the Blue Ridge Mountains. There is an army, intact, in the Carolinas. Joe Johnston's army. If we can reach them, we'll keep fighting there."

"I don't have enough to feed all your men, Captain. Some potatoes, a little horse meat."

"Probably isn't time to eat, anyway. I believe there to be Yankee cavalry in those woods. You had better leave."

"Leave?" The thought had not occurred to Talcott before this moment. "I cannot. I will not. This is my home, sir. The Yankees would not dare harm me or my daughter." But there was something less than complete conviction in his voice.

"Perhaps not," conceded Dalton. "Some of their units are well disciplined. Some are less so. I have heard reports of pillaging. . . . "

He glanced at Margaret again, and she saw the concern in those arresting blue eyes.

"Besides," said Talcott, "I have wounded soldiers in here. I have no means to transport them—and some of them could not be moved anyway."

"Leave the wounded," said Dalton curtly. "Their best hope is a Yankee hospital, in any event."

"You would leave your own comrades-in-arms to the enemy?"

"Yes," rasped Dalton, and pointed to the men in the

road. "Getting these men out of the Yankee trap—that's my responsibility." He glanced at the old soldier. "Want to come along?"

The old veteran shook his head. "My war's over, I reckon, Cap'n. I'll stick with the kid here. Mebbe I'll be able to get him home all in one piece."

"Good luck to you."

"I will not turn tail and run from Yankees," said Talcott.

Dalton glanced east again. Margaret read the impotent rage on his bearded, haggard face, mixed with a calm deliberation.

"That is your choice," he said, and by his tone it was clear he thought it the wrong choice. He touched his hat as he looked at Margaret again. "Best of luck." He was directing these good wishes to her, not Talcott. She wanted to beg him not to leave. She felt suddenly very much in jeopardy, and for some reason she knew she would be safe as long as he was around. In fact, she had a hunch that the only safe place in this world turned upside down was with Captain John Dalton.

But of course she did not call out, and Dalton swung long legs over the broken gate and was back in the road again, barking another order, and the soldier-scarecrows got to their feet somehow and followed him on down the road, and as they passed they smiled at the people on the veranda, and a few tipped their hats, and Margaret reflected bitterly on the unfairness of life, because it was so unfair that the Confederacy was lost, even with such men as these to fight for her. In a perfect world such men would triumph, and it would have nothing to do with whether their cause was just.

2

Walking away from the Talcott house, Dalton had an urge to look back, and fought against it savagely. He wanted to rest his eyes on Margaret again. But what good would that do? Looking at her made him think about all of life's might-have-beens, which now, thanks to the war, would never be. By her very presence she made him contemplate the future, something he had tried these past four years as a soldier to avoid. There seemed little point in thinking about the future now.

Still, he couldn't eradicate her from his thoughts. There was just something special about her. Somehow he knew with absolute conviction that in another time and another place they would have been friends, if not more, and he wanted to go back and find out all about her, and forget about this damned war, pretend it never happened. He cursed himself for a fool. A chance meeting, a few pleasantries exchanged, a significant glance or two, and Margaret Talcott, a woman he had seen for five minutes and would never see again from this moment to the grave, had moved right to the top of his list of life's might-have-beens. It was absurd, of course, but Dalton was resigned to the fact that he would never forget her, she would haunt him forever.

"That's what we are fighting for, Jack."

Dalton hadn't realized that Clement Pease was walking beside him. Pease was a lieutenant. He and Dalton were the only commissioned officers remaining in the company. A short, slight, and rather bookish individual, Pease had arrived as a replacement in '62, just in time for Second Manassas. He'd been a clerk in a mercantile back in Montgomery before signing up. Seeing him for the first time, Dalton hadn't thought much of his chances for survival. Pease just didn't look like much of a soldier. But he had proved Dalton wrong. He was smart, brave, and absolutely unflappable under fire. The men trusted him. Dalton had entered the Thirty-second Alabama with five friends. All of them were dead now, with the exception of Jethro Cutshaw, who was back in Alabama with one leg and only the thumb and forefinger remaining on his left hand. Dalton had vowed not to make any more friends— there just wasn't any future in it—but Pease had managed to worm his way into the role in spite of Dalton's best efforts.

"The ladies of the South," said Pease, perceiving that his previous remark had gone uncomprehended. "They represent the very best of our culture. Grace, beauty, refinement, compassion. They bring to mind the cloying sweetness of magnolia blossoms, the seductive rustle of silk, the . . . "

"Shut up, Clement." Sometimes Dalton couldn't tell whether Pease was serious or just pulling his leg. The man had a peculiar sense of humor. He always seemed to view life through the slightly skewed lens of his own private irony.

"I mean it, Jack. Like that one back there—all that grace, beauty, and courage wrapped up in one beguiling package. She represents a culture, a way of life, that is distinctly different from any other the world has ever seen.

That's what we are fighting for, isn't it? To preserve that way of life? The Yankees have never understood. We are as different from them as day from night. It's simply a fluke of history that we are part of the same nation. It should never have been so, and we were just trying to set things to rights. And even though it looks like we will be one nation again, nothing really will change, no matter how hard they try to impose their culture on us. There will always be a South, and no one will ever mistake it for any other section of the country."

Dalton didn't know what to say. Pease was a loquacious soul. He liked to air his thoughts, or hear himself talk, and many was the time Dalton could scarcely follow his train of thought. Sometimes he made perfect sense, sometimes not.

"Isn't that what you are fighting for, Jack? Haven't you been to war for the sake of that girl back there? Even though you never knew before today that she existed?"

"I don't know," said Dalton. "I don't remember why I went to war. That was a long time ago."

It was true, he didn't remember, and realizing that caught him by surprise. Those glory days seemed like another life, another world.

"I suppose I'll go back to being a clerk," said Pease. "What are you going to do?"

"Damn it, lower your voice. You talk as though the war is over. The men don't need to hear that kind of talk from one of their own officers."

"But the war *is* over, Jack. They know that. Just look at them. You can see it written all over their faces. Look at them and tell me you don't see it."

Dalton glanced over his shoulder. All he saw were grim warriors, men who could march further and fight harder than any other band of men in the history of warfare, men who were almost superhuman in their endurance and bravery, men who would charge hell at his order, and do it with unquenchable élan.

"No," he said. "I don't see it."

"Because you don't want to. Mark my words, Jack, General Lee will surrender before the week is out."

Dalton wanted to grab Pease and choke him until his eyes popped out of their sockets.

"Maybe he will," he growled. "But that doesn't mean the war is over for me. It isn't over for me until I decide it's over. And it's not over as long as there is one man willing to fight and die for what he thinks is right."

"God, Jack. You have the zeal of a seventeenth-century Scots Covenanter, I'll give you that. But you said you don't even remember what you're fighting for."

"I said I didn't know why I went to war. I'm fighting now to stay alive. Now shut up."

The road took them through a strip of trees and across a stone bridge which spanned a babbling brook. Beyond the bridge the road turned up an incline and left the cool, green shade of the trees before straightening out to cut like an arrow between two fields. At least they had once been fields. Now there was nothing but corn stubble on one side and hard-packed red mud on the other. Dalton figured this property also belonged to Talcott. Once, no doubt, fine crops had flourished here, tended by Talcott's field hands. The slaves were long gone. Some had run to the Yankees, others had run away from them. The Yankees used "contraband" slaves to build earthworks and dig latrines and, it was said, often treated the slaves worse than their former masters had done, giving them work that the white soldiers considered themselves too good to do.

For Dalton, the war had never been about slavery. Like the majority of white Southerners he had never owned a slave and never intended to. He didn't much care for the concept behind slavery. Many slaveholders didn't like it either. But a place like Talcott's had needed a lot of workers, and slaves had been the only available labor source. Talcott had lost his labor source, and now his fields lay in ruins. But that really didn't matter anymore, decided Dalton. Talcott probably wouldn't even own ruined fields for much longer. To the victors go the spoils; after the Yankee soldiers would come the Yankee landgrabbers. Men like Talcott, made destitute by four long years of war, would not be able to pay taxes on their land, and the land would be taken away from them, and the only people who would have the money to buy land anymore would be the Yankees. Dalton could confidently predict the future for men like Talcott, even while his own future remained obscure. His thoughts naturally turned to Margaret again, and he wondered what she would do when the Yankees took the land away.

Then he heard the gunfire—a single shot, followed by a ragged volley, the familiar crackling of repeating rifles. It came from back down the road. The Talcott house. Dalton and the rest of the company halted in their tracks. He listened hard for the sound of more shooting. Ominous silence. Turning, he saw that Pease and the others were watching him intently. Everyone knew what the shooting signified. Bluecoats. Only the Yanks had repeating rifles.

"Lieutenant, hold the men here while I go take a look."

Pease nodded, looking as though he had known exactly what Dalton would do even before the captain had spoken.

Dalton strode briskly back down the road and into the trees. He wanted to run, because he was sick with worry about Margaret, but held himself in check. When he reached the bridge he could see the Talcott house, a hundred yards away. And what he saw made his blood run cold.

Yankee cavalry.

A hundred blue-clad horse soldiers at least, swarming like locusts around the big red-brick house. A couple of riderless horses were running in the ruined field across the road from the house. Dalton could guess what that meant. Two Yankee cavalrymen dead or wounded. He recalled seeing the Tarpley rifle next to the old, shoeless Confederate on the veranda. The Yankee cavalry had come out of the woods to the east and someone had taken potshots at them with that rifle. Dalton couldn't believe the old veteran had done anything so stupid. Maybe Talcott had done it.

Hearing someone on the run behind him, Dalton whirled, his nerves on edge. It was Sergeant Muldoon. The stocky Irishman's face was as red as his carrot-colored beard.

"The lieutenant sent me along to look out for you, Cap'n." Muldoon grinned. He glanced beyond Dalton at the bluecoats, and his grin tightened, turned wolfish. "Well, now. This is our lucky day."

"Go back and bring up the others, Sergeant."

Muldoon's grin got bigger. The Irishman was tired of running. But he was never too tired for a good donnybrook. "Yes, sir!"

"Bring them quietly."

Dalton returned to his search for any sign of Margaret as Muldoon lumbered back up the road. Several Federals were dismounted and on the veranda. Others had disappeared into the house. Many milled around on their horses in the speckled shade of the sassafras trees in front of the house. Others had circled around to cover the back. No one was paying the strip of trees along the creek any attention. Standing in the deep afternoon shade, Dalton figured he was safe from discovery even if they had been looking in his direction.

Then he saw Talcott—being manhandled out of the house by a pair of Billy Yanks. They threw him down into the dust at the foot of the veranda steps. But Talcott was too proud a man to stay down for long. Pouncing indignantly to his feet, he lunged foolishly at the nearest mounted soldier and wrenched the startled man's carbine from his grasp.

"No," said Dalton, a hoarse whisper.

Five or six guns spoke at once. Talcott didn't stand a chance. It was suicide. But a man like Talcott would not tolerate such rough treatment, especially at the hands of Yankees. He didn't live long enough to fire a shot. As he fell, riddled with bullets, Dalton cursed him silently. The man was so damned worried about his own pride that he had forgotten about his daughter. What good would he do Margaret dead?

By this time Pease and the rest of the company had arrived. Dalton took them across the bridge and dispersed them into the fringe of trees on both sides of the road, until only he, Lieutenant Pease, and Sergeant Muldoon stood in the road. Appropriating the lieutenant's prized fieldglass, he kept looking for Margaret, desperation growing inside him. He heard more shots from inside the house. The sound made his shoulders twitch involuntarily. Someone hurled a chair through a window. He saw what he thought was the flicker of flame through another window.

"What are they doing?" asked Pease.

"Shooting the wounded and burning the house," said Dalton, his voice hollow.

Pease stared at him in disbelief. "Surely you're . . . "

"Damn," muttered Dalton.

A soldier was dragging Margaret out the back door of

the house. She was fighting like a wildcat, and he struck her, exasperated, with a closed fist, knocking her to the ground. Six cavalrymen were present at the rear of the house, with not an officer among them. Two dismounted and converged on Margaret. They were laughing. Dalton swept the fieldglass to the cluster of horse soldiers in front of the house, saw some officers, realized they were completely unaware of what was transpiring behind the house.

"What's going on?" queried Pease. "What are they doing to her?"

Dalton swung the fieldglass back to the scene at the rear of the house. A roar of sheer rage welled up in his throat, but he beat it down. Margaret was still on the ground, and the three dismounted soldiers were looming over her. One of them nudged her with his boot, leering. Dalton tasted bile, like copper, on his tongue. Margaret got to her feet. One of the cavalrymen shoved her into the rough embrace of another. She clawed the man's face and tried to escape him. He held on, and her dress tore at the shoulder. . . .

Dalton hurled the fieldglass down and started walking up the road, fumbling in a blind rage with the flap of the holster at his side, dragging out the Whitney revolver.

"Jack!"

This was Pease, but Dalton could not hear him. He pulled the Whitney's trigger, knowing the range was too great for accuracy and not giving a damn, but the percussion revolver dry-fired. Dalton cursed furiously, tried again. The Whitney had never done this. Why now? What cruel fate was this? Another misfire.

Pease picked up the fieldglass, brushed it off, and glanced, sardonic as always, at Muldoon.

"I suppose we had better go along with him, Sergeant. He might need us. The odds are a little long, even for Dalton."

Muldoon was ecstatic. "Yes, sir!"

Third time was the charm for Dalton. The Whitney barked, and hard on the heels of the gunshot came the Rebel Yell, issuing from thirty parched throats as the company surged out of the trees to sweep across the dusty road and the dead fields towards the Talcott house and one more battle.

3

The Rebel Yell startled Dalton as much as it did the Federals. Witnessing the molestation of Margaret Talcott at the hands of the horse soldiers had made him forget what he had not forgotten in four years—that he had the responsibility of command. The war had abruptly become a personal thing—solely between him and those three Yankee cavalrymen menacing Margaret—and in his outrage he had charged into the open with but one intention, to kill the offending bluecoats, and without giving thought to his own safety or the well-being of his company.

What they did came as no surprise to him. The odds were long, but they had always been so, and that sort of thing didn't concern them in the least. These past few days, ever since the retreat from Richmond began, they had seen other units simply dissolve into non-existence, as men made up their minds that there were more important things than the Cause, things like finding food and getting home. It had occurred to Dalton, a recurring anxiety, that his company might do the same at some point, without warning.

But now, at this moment, his heart swelled with pride

as, to a man, the company charged out of the trees to join him in his reckless assault, in a sense redeeming him, by making his fight their own. He was ashamed, then, of the doubts he had entertained about these men. They were fierce in their loyalty to him, and he knew they were risking death this time not for the Confederacy but solely for his sake. They were buying into his very personal fight.

The totally unexpected appearance of Dalton's Confederates momentarily threw the Federal cavalry into confusion. In those key first few minutes the officer in charge, a quite capable major who was fortunate enough to have learned his craft under the auspices of John Buford, one of the Union's finest cavalry leaders, lost control of his troopers. It was every man for himself. A few, completely rattled, turned their horses around and fled, seeing a division of graycoats where there was only an understrength company. They were unnerved by that hellish yell, not to mention the buzzing and whining and cracking of bullets. Others spurred their horses forward, impetuously charging the Confederates, returning fire. Still others, those made of sterner and more rational stuff, dismounted and prepared to stand their ground against the Rebel onslaught.

The major was a veteran. He knew that if there was one thing this war had demonstrated it was that cavalry fought best on foot. Using horses to get from one place to another in a hurry was one thing. Fighting on horseback was something else entirely. Cavalry fighting cavalry made sense, although it rarely happened. But against well-trained enemy foot soldiers in anything like equal numbers, cavalrymen invariably got the worst of it. Having learned this cardinal rule, the major tried to get his men dismounted and in ranks. Meanwhile, the dozen or so hotheads who were galloping into the teeth of the Rebel charge, inspired perhaps by the example of George

Armstrong Custer, the dashing beau ideal of Union horse soldiers, were cut down in short order.

The Confederates rushed onward, each soldier stopping to fire and reload, then to run a few yards further before stopping to fire again and reload again. They knew better than to charge in neat, orderly ranks. Covering a front of about a hundred yards, they were well dispersed. Almost all of them were veterans of at least several major campaigns, and they knew how to make their ammunition count.

The Talcott house was ablaze now, tongues of flame flicking out of the doors and windows, billowing grayish-black smoke and preventing the Federals from taking cover anywhere near it. The Yankee major tried to get his men arranged into orderly ranks. He wanted them to be able to fire a full volley into the Confederates. While every third man took charge of his horse and two others, the rest of the horse soldiers knelt in a nice, neat, blue line across the road. They were armed with the new Spencer carbines, and this gave them added firepower, as the Spencer sported a seven-shot magazine.

Dalton realized his men would not stand a chance once the bluecoats got organized and commenced a sustained firing. There was no cover to be had, so he shouted his men to get down. Pease and Muldoon, to the left and right of him, relayed the order. The brass-throated Irish sergeant was particularly useful for transmitting orders in the din of battle. His stentorian voice could drown out a regimental band. The Confederates dropped to the ground just in time. The Federal major gave his men the command to open fire. The ranks of blue-clad soldiers momentarily disappeared behind a line of muzzle flash that resembled a horizontal bolt of lightning. Belly-down on the hard-ribbed clay of the field, Dalton was half-blinded by dirt thrown into his eyes by the impact of the bullets smacking into the ground. But most of the Yankee bullets flew harmlessly over the heads of Dalton and his men, making a wicked cracking sound as they passed.

Dalton had fired three rounds at the cavalrymen molesting Margaret—to no avail, as far as he could tell. Now he emptied the Whitney into the Federal line. His men returned fire, too, to good effect. Nine or ten horse soldiers fell. A bullet struck the major from his saddle. He had thought it best to remain mounted and in full view for the sake of his command's morale. Now, his death demoralized the Federals. Their fire diminished notice-ably. Dalton's battle instincts told him they were faltering. He had a decision to make. His men could not hold out for long in this position. He was painfully aware of the fact that not a soul in the company had more than a dozen rounds of ammunition in his shot pouch. The element of surprise had brought them to within thirty yards of the house. They had to go the rest of the way. If they stayed where they were or tried to get back to the trees they would be cut down.

It was now or never. Dalton leaped to his feet, drew his sword and, pointing it at the Federals, turned to his men.

"Let's see 'em run one more time, boys!" .

A shout arose from every throat in the company. To a man the Confederates stood and plunged ahead. The Spencers crackled like heat lightning. Men fell to either side of Dalton. But he did not waver in his resolve, and his men stayed with him, and the only way the Federals could stop them was to cut them down, every one. Instead, the horse soldiers broke. A few at first, unnerved, ran for their horses. Then the whole line was up and run-ning. A couple paused to retrieve their commander's body. They were shot down. The rest galloped away, in full and frantic flight, making for the treeline to the east, pursued by the jeers and bullets of the handful of Confederates still standing.

Dalton made for the back of the house, where he had last seen Margaret. His heart seemed firmly lodged in his throat, and he could hardly breathe. He found her on the ground, huddled behind the body of a dead Yankee cavalryman. At first he thought she was dead. But as his shadow passed over her she opened her eyes and saw him and stood, and Dalton felt like laughing, so great was his relief.

"Are you hurt?"

She shook her head. He held out his hand. Without hesitation she took it. Her dress was torn at the shoulder, and she tried to hold it together with her other hand. Her hand felt very small and delicate in his, and her touch sent a kind of lightning through his body, a sensation he could feel all the way down to the soles of his feet. She looked at the body of the dead cavalryman, then at the burning house, then at Dalton, and he couldn't fathom her expression.

"Is my father dead?"

Dalton nodded, expecting her to fall apart at the news, but she surprised him. She was hit hard, but he marvelled at how well she maintained her composure. The tears welled up in her eyes but she did not let them escape. She gripped his hand very tightly. He didn't utter any words of consolation. For him, death had become such a commonplace that it hardly bore mentioning, and he had forgotten all those things one was supposed to say to another who had lost a loved one.

With a rending crash part of the roof caved in, and Dalton looked up to see a huge pillar of flame shoot skyward. In a matter of hours the house would be little more than a scorched shell of bricks. They could feel the searing blast of heat from the raging conflagration, and Dalton led her by the hand a safe distance away. This brought them near a wounded horse soldier. He was curled up on his side, arms wrapped tightly around his midsection, and Dalton knew he had been gut shot, a mortal wound. The soldier was shaking violently, uncontrollably, and he was white as a sheet. Looking up at Dalton he tried to speak, but coughed up blood, and began to weep.

"Can't we do something for him?" asked Margaret.

"Isn't this one of the men who . . ." He didn't know quite how to put it.

"Yes, he is."

"And you still want to help him?"

"Yes."

He shook his head, bewildered. There wasn't a trace of compassion on his gaunt, bearded face.

"There's nothing we can do for him. Except maybe shoot him. Put him out of his misery, the way you would a horse with a broken leg. A bullet in the brain. Otherwise, he'll die slow."

"You're trying to shock me, Captain. You are a hard man. I know. It's the war that has done this to you. Made you the kind of man you are. I don't hold it against you."

"Maybe."

She looked sadly at the dying cavalryman. "The war made him do what he did, too."

Dalton just gazed at her with unabashed admiration.

"Jack!"

Pease appeared through a drifting wall of smoke from the burning house. Seeing the lieutenant brought Dalton to his senses, and he was instantly assailed by conscience-searing guilt. He knew what was coming.

With scarcely a glance at Margaret, Pease, all business now, said, "We lost nine men killed. Five wounded, three of whom won't be able to get very far on foot."

Nine men! Dalton winced. Nine gallant soldiers had

perished on his account. Always before, when he led men
into battle, into the valley of the shadow, he had done so
for the Cause. But this time it had been for the sake of a
woman. He didn't hold Margaret responsible, but rather
blamed himself, even as he knew that he would do the
same again if the situation arose. There was nothing else he
could have done. He could see that Pease believed that,
because Pease could read his guilt. It was ironic, mused
Dalton, that only a short while ago the lieutenant had
waxed eloquent about Margaret Talcott being the living
symbol of everything they had been fighting and dying for.

"Some of the men are catching up as many horses as
they can," continued Pease. "We can put the men who
can't walk in the saddle." Again he glanced at Margaret.
"And we'll get one for you, too, ma'am, if you like."

Dalton turned to her. He wanted to ask her to come
with him, but of course he couldn't do that. He had no
idea where he was going, what would become of him. A
man who has no future has very little to offer, and no
right to ask another to share in it. Besides, she probably
had family somewhere. . . .

"Thank you," she told Pease, and then, to Dalton, "Do
we have time to bury my father?"

"Those Yankee horse soldiers will realize sooner or
later that they outnumber us four to one."

She nodded.

"Clement, make sure every round of ammunition is
taken off these Yankees. We're probably going to need it."

Pease nodded and went away. The day was long past
when he had last saluted Dalton. It wasn't out of lack of
respect, but rather dispensing with unnecessary protocol
between friends. Dalton didn't give it a thought.

"What about your dead, Captain?"

"It's a long way from Alabama," he said, bleakly sur-
veying the field of battle.

"I don't believe I understand."

He shook his head. "We leave them lie where they fell. Someone will come along eventually and give them a decent burial. Your father, too. I'm sorry, Miss Talcott, but we are on the run."

"Please call me Margaret. As for my father, don't apologize. I think somehow I knew he would not survive the war. He was so . . . bitter. You see, my brother lost his life at Gettysburg, and Father could not bring himself to forgive the Yankees. I dreaded their coming, because I was afraid that something like this would happen. I didn't know what he would do when a Yankee set foot on Talcott land."

"Did your father fire that first shot?"

"Yes. He took the old soldier's gun."

"That was a damn fool thing to do."

Her smile was tolerant. "I know. Now he's dead, and Lucius, and all those poor, brave, wounded Confederates. And all these other men. And what about what you did, Captain? Coming to my rescue, a knight in gray armor. Was that a damn fool thing to do, too?"

"I see they've got some horses," said Dalton, turning quickly away. "We'd better get moving."

"Where?"

"West. I want to reach the Appomattox River by nightfall. Of course, I'll see to it that you get safely to wherever . . . "

"I have no place to go now," she said. "No one who cares. I'll go with you."

4

They reached the Appomattox River an hour before sundown, arriving at High Bridge to find the span and the road leading to it clogged with the remnants of the Army of Northern Virginia. There had been a battle here that very afternoon. Federal infantry had tried to slice through the Confederates and destroy the bridge before Lee's army could escape across it. Yankee cavalry had come to the rescue of that infantry unit as it was hit hard by Tom Rosser's Rebel horsemen. Close and bloody work with sabers and pistols followed, and the issue was in doubt until the Thirty-fifth Virginia Battalion appeared to drive the bluecoats from the field.

There was crowding and confusion at the bridge, which arched across the steep bluffs flanking the river. Dalton led his company into this miscellaneous crowd creeping with agonizing slowness across the span. Margaret Talcott and the three seriously wounded men were mounted. Though she was an accomplished rider, she was content to let Dalton lead her horse. From the east and north and south came the sounds of sporadic engagements, the crackle of musketry, the boom of cannons. The Yankees were pressing hard on all sides. But there was no panic in the

Confederate ranks. Dusk was soon upon them, and night was their ally, as it is for all fugitives.

That night they finally got across High Bridge and camped a mile or so down the road to Farmville. Muldoon and a couple of others ventured off to try to find some food. The Irishman was far and away the most accomplished scavenger the company had ever known, and he did not fail this time, returning with some middlings of meat, corn, hardtack, and even a jar of molasses. Better yet, he brought an empty caisson. The wounded could henceforth be transported on this, with two of the horses attached to the tongue of the conveyance. Dalton hoped to find a hospital train tomorrow near Farmville where, it was said, General Lee had made his headquarters for the night.

Stragglers and scavengers from other units passed through their camp into the early hours of the morning, looking for food, whiskey, medicine, ammunition, horses—anything they could beg, borrow, or steal. Dalton made sure that their four horses were carefully guarded.

All about them in the darkness flickered dozens of other campfires. Dalton took a stroll, hoping against hope that he could find at least a portion of the Thirty-second Alabama. All he found were groups of soldiers lying on the hard ground more like dead men than living. There was very little talking, no music, no laughter. Neither were there any sentries. He could find not a single officer above his own rank. By the time he got back to his company he had reached the conclusion that the Army of Northern Virginia had almost ceased to exist as a fighting force. In its place was a rabble of weary, hungry individuals looking out for themselves. It would be the end of everything if the Yankees made an all-out attack now. He was depressed by what he had seen, and Pease could tell.

"It's bad, isn't it," said the lieutenant.

Dalton nodded.

"I'm telling you, Jack, the war is over."

"As long as General Lee wants to continue I will follow him. I have followed him for four years, and I can't stop now."

"The Yankees will cut us off eventually. We used to march rings around them. Not anymore. General Lee will have to surrender, sooner or later. Then we can all go home."

"You'll go home, Clement."

"What about you?"

"There is nothing for me back in Alabama."

"So what will you do?"

Dalton glanced across the camp at Margaret. She was curled up on the ground, asleep, near the campfire. The night was cool and damp.

"I'm not sure," he replied, and went over to drape his tunic over the sleeping woman.

Morning broke with the sound of guns back in the vicinity of High Bridge. Hundreds of Confederates emerged from the woods and struck out west along the Farmville road, not because anyone had ordered them to march west, but because that was the only direction left open to them.

Entering Farmville a couple of hours later, Dalton spotted General Lee. He was washing his face in a basin of water on the porch of a house at the east end of town. Of medium height and stocky build, the general's face was bronzed by long exposure to the elements. His manners and bearing were always as impeccable as his uniform. He was the ultimate Southern gentleman-cavalier. As he dried his snow-white beard with a towel, an officer Dalton recognized as Brigadier General Henry Wise arrived in a mud-splattered uniform. Lee gestured at the dusty stream of soldiers plodding along the road in front of the house.

"You will take command of these forces, General Wise. Make all the stragglers fall into your ranks."

"I will try, sir. But it isn't the men who are deserting the ranks, but the officers who are deserting the men. The officers are responsible for this."

Lee's face was a stony mask. "Are you referring to any specific officer?"

"General Bushrod Johnson fled the battle at Sayler's Creek. I understand he reported to you that the entire division was cut to pieces. I can guarantee, sir, that my brigade is very much intact. Johnson is a damned, dirty coward."

"Are you aware, General Wise, that you are liable to court martial and execution for insubordination and disrespect toward your commanding officer? You could be shot for what you have just said."

"Shot?" Wise grinned like a hungry wolf. "You can hardly afford to shoot the men who fight for cursing those who run away. But go ahead and shoot me if you must, sir. You might as well. I expect a Yankee will do the job before the day is out, in any case."

Lee smiled. "Quite right. I cannot afford to shoot you, Henry. How do you see our situation?"

"Nothing remains but to send the men home in time for spring plowing. The army is whipped, General. These men have withstood more than I thought mere flesh and blood was capable of enduring."

"What would the Confederacy think of me if I did as you suggest and disbanded the army?"

"What Confederacy?" asked Wise. "What army? There has been no Confederacy for almost a year now. These men fight for you, not their country. They have fought for a long time without pay or clothes or care of any kind. And they will still fight and die for you. Forgive me for being blunt, sir, but now is no time for mincing words.

The blood of every man who is killed from this time forward is on your head."

Carried along in the plodding stream of men, Dalton heard no more of the conversation, but what he had heard convinced him that his doubts of last night were justified. The army was finished. As the day wore on a subtle change was wrought in him, brought on by what he had seen and heard. Always he had been diligent in his concern for the men under his command, but that concern had remained second to his foremost purpose in life, fighting and defeating the enemy. For that reason he could lead men to their deaths in battle—men he cared about. Now, though, fighting and defeating the Yankees ceased to be a motivating factor. His sole purpose from then on was to save his men.

Despite the order Lee had given General Wise, Dalton saw no evidence of an attempt to reorganize the rabble into a fighting force. He heard that they had tried to burn the High Bridge, and another span across the Appomattox River, before the Yankees could cross in force. The former was successfully put to the torch, but the bluecoats hastened to seize the latter, driving off a weak Confederate rear guard, and extinguishing the blaze. This meant there would be no respite for the weary Rebels on the roads west. With the enemy nipping at its heels, the remnants of a once-proud army, a swarm of men and wagons and worn-out mules and horses, continued to creep towards the Blue Ridge Mountains. Skirmishes erupted on a regular basis on the flanks. Now and then Federal artillery fire came crashing suddenly and fearsomely down upon a section of crowded road. Dead men, dead horses, and blazing wagons were always the grim harvest.

It was Friday, April 7, and on that night most of the ragged columns did not stop. Dalton pressed on. One of the severely wounded men riding on the caisson died a little after nightfall. Dalton left two men behind to bury him. He did not expect to see these two again, and shook their hands, advising them to try to make their way home as best they could.

He could not know that at nine o'clock that night a Federal officer, General Seth Williams of Grant's staff, appeared under a flag of truce at a Confederate picket line north of the road. General James Longstreet sent one of his aides, Colonel Herman Perry, to hear the Yankee emissary out. Williams offered Perry a pocket flask of brandy by way of a preliminary courtesy, but the Confederate declined this generosity with stiff cordiality.

"I am here to receive your communications, sir," said Perry. "I cannot properly accept your kind offer."

Williams handed him a letter. "This is from General Grant, addressed to General Lee. Please see that he receives it immediately."

Perry took the letter to Longstreet, and then on to Lee's headquarters. The letter read:

General R. E. Lee
Commanding C.S. Army

General:
The results of the last week must convince you of the hopelessness of further resistance on the part of the Army of Northern Virginia. I regard it as my duty to shift from myself the responsibility of any further effusion of blood, by asking you to surrender.

Very respectfully, your obedient servant
U. S. Grant
Lt. General Commanding,
Armies of the United States

"Not yet," said Lee softly, after reading the letter, and immediately sat down to write a reply. Then he gave the order to continue the retreat.

Next morning the rains came.

The Confederates' starving mules and horses could not drag the wagons and the cannon through the mud. The guns were buried, the wagons and caissons burned. Dalton witnessed further evidence of demoralization and disintegration. The ditches became littered with discarded muskets and small arms, thrown down by soldiers who had made up their minds that they would fight no more. He saw thieves cut the bridles of horses from the wrists of officers asleep by the wayside. Others began to range far afield to loot nearby farms—an act that would have earned them a firing squad had they been apprehended. Small groups drifted off into the woods to await the Federals, intending to surrender. Officers turned a blind eye to this steady attrition in the ranks. Dalton noted proudly that not a single man in his own company turned up missing.

That evening they reached Appomattox Court House. Dalton led his exhausted crew into some pines near a creek called Rocky Run, and found a good, secluded campsite in some broom grass hard by an old split-rail fence which provided kindling. The rain had finally slackened. Again Muldoon led a detail off to find food, returning with ash cakes and a little coffee and tobacco. He swore on his mother's grave to Dalton that a farmer and his wife had freely offered him these things.

By the light of the campfire Dalton took a good, hard look at his men. Their clothes were tattered and caked with mud. Their eyes were sunk deep in their sockets, and their faces were terribly gaunt. They looked to him more dead than alive. Their endurance astonished him, even as he gave no thought to his own, and he wondered how much further they could go without rest. He did not think it would be much further. As for Margaret, she endured as gamely as the veterans. He offered to escort her to the nearest farm, where she would be safe. His heart wasn't in the offer, and he was relieved when she would have none of it.

Pease took a stroll and came back wearing a troubled expression. Dalton knew things had to be bad if Clement Pease looked worried.

"I came upon part of Kershaw's division," said Pease. "Two hundred men. That's all that's left—out of a whole division! They say there is Yankee cavalry across our path. They've swung around in front of us, Jack. Cut us off. No escape. They say that in the morning General Lee will give the order to attack and try to break through."

They went to sleep to the dreadful, even though by now familiar, music of the relentless Federal artillery.

5

It was Sunday, April 9.

There was a light frost on the ground at daybreak, but the sky was a clear azure blue, and it was soon quite warm. The rising sun swiftly dispelled the mist which had gathered in the low places.

At first light a vigorous and sustained roll of musketry erupted in the west, and Dalton knew then that Pease had heard right—the Yankees had finally gotten across their path in force and were trying to block the army's escape. This caused no little consternation among the Confederates. Yankee artillery boomed, very close now. Dalton heard the cannonballs ripping through the tops of the trees, and saw them strike less than two hundred yards away, on the other side of the road. Trees exploded. Great geysers of earth shot upwards. The ground shuddered. Men ran for their lives. Pease suggested they leave, post haste, but Dalton kept his men in place, watching the explosions. Acrid smoke drifted across the road into their camp. In a matter of minutes it was over—the Federals shifted their aim to a spot along the road a quarter-mile further west. This was what Dalton had thought they would do, and why he had held his company in their camp.

"I think they've bagged us," said Pease. "What do we do now, Jack? Which way do we go?"

"West."

"But the Yankees are in the west now, too."

"Most of them are still behind us. I figure they sent their cavalry around to cut us off, and I have a feeling General Lee will try to punch through. We're not far from the mountains now, Clement. If we can get to Lynchburg and the railroad there . . . "

Pease just smirked and shook his head. "They've finally cornered the Gray Fox, but you're just too stubborn to admit it."

They arrived at the hamlet of Appomattox Court House in less than an hour. On the outskirts of town they saw an entire squadron of Confederate cavalry in a field, motionless, asleep in their saddles. The troopers and their horses both had their heads down, as if they were all praying. Noting the sorry condition of the horses, Dalton was surprised they were still standing.

The streets of town were filled with Confederate soldiers. They stood or sat around in apparent indifference to the world around them. Sporadic gunfire still sounded from the woodlands west of town. Dalton found a captain from the Forty-fifth North Carolina, who told him what had transpired.

Brigadier General Bryan Grimes was commanding the foremost Confederate division. A fiery North Carolinian, he had led his men in a furious attack on the Yankee positions flung across the army's path, driving them back, capturing several hundred prisoners and two artillery pieces. He sent word to his corps commander, John B. Gordon, to announce that the road to Lynchburg was, for the moment, open. But Gordon could not take advantage of this opportunity, for Federal infantry had appeared in large numbers to the north of him. He reluctantly ordered Grimes to withdraw to Appomattox Court House. At first Grimes refused to obey. He was convinced that Gordon did not fully understand the situation. The door was thrown open. The army could escape, if it acted with dispatch. He went to Gordon himself, and was dismayed to learn that Gordon had just received word from Lee's headquarters that the Army of Northern Virginia was going to be surrendered. Recovering from his shock and chagrin, Grimes became irate, and vowed to take his division and fight his way out. But Gordon persuaded him that to do so would reflect badly on General Lee, who was even then in the process of giving his solemn word to the Yankees that all hostilities would end.

Dalton had feared for several days that this dreadful moment was imminent. At first he was stunned, empty. Then he felt anger, shame, and relief, all at the same time.

"The race is not always won," remarked Pease, "by those with the longest legs. We could have whipped them, Jack. We could have, if it had been anything close to an equal fight."

Dalton just gave him a blank stare.

"My Gawd," muttered Sergeant Muldoon. "This is a bloody black day, indeed. What now, Cap'n? What happens now?"

"I have no idea," confessed Dalton. "I suppose we will find a place to make ourselves comfortable and just wait and see."

They found a good place, near a two-story, red-brick house close to the courthouse, where locust trees provided some pleasant shade, and they stretched out on the cool, luxuriant grass, and Margaret sat down next to Dalton and put a gentle hand on his arm.

"Every end marks a new beginning," she said.

He nodded, but said nothing.

A man came from the house to bring them a bucket of sweet well water with a ladle in it.

"Name's Wilmer McLean," he said. "Used to have a farm up Manassas way. After they fought two battles in my fields I moved my family down here, lock, stock, and barrel. Figured this to be a nice, quiet place. Didn't think the war would follow me here. Guess I was wrong."

"There is nothing else for me to do," said Lee, upon receiving Gordon's report of large numbers of Yankee infantry to the north and west, "but to go see General Grant."

"What will history say?" asked one of his distraught staff officers.

"We were overwhelmed by sheer numbers," replied Lee, struggling valiantly to maintain his composure. "Believe me, gentlemen, when I say that I would prefer to die a thousand deaths than to surrender this army."

Grim silence reigned as Lee, in the Grimsley saddle of his horse, the dappled gray called Traveler, scanned Gordon's lines with his fieldglasses from the vantage point of a pine-bristling hill. He was clad in an immaculate, new uniform, with golden spurs strapped to high-polished boots. As he studied the field of battle, Generals Longstreet and Mahone arrived. Longstreet, who knew Lee better than anyone in the army, could see beneath his commander's brave and dignified bearing to the man's anguished soul.

"There seems to be a considerable force of the enemy in front of us," said Lee. "I am considering surrender. Your opinion would be most welcome."

"Would the sacrifice of this army help the Cause?"

"I do not see how it would."

"Then the situation speaks for itself," said Longstreet, with characteristic bluntness.

Lee next went to E. P. Alexander, an old friend, and the officer in charge of the army's artillery.

"We have two choices," said Alexander. "Surrender, or scatter and rally to General Johnston down in North Carolina. I suggest the latter course of action. If you surrender, every other army will be so demoralized that it will lay down its weapons."

"How many of our men do you suppose could get out of this trap?"

"At least half of them. Perhaps as many as two thirds. We would scatter like rabbits into the woods. They could not catch us all."

"But the men would be without rations, and be under no discipline."

"I'm afraid that is the case with many of them now."

"Yes. And I have had deeply disturbing reports of some of them preying on our own civilians. If I took your suggestion and dispersed the army some of them would turn to robbery. You younger men might be able to go bushwhacking. But the only proper course for me is surrender."

"Of course, General, you must consider what is best for the men, and decide not only for yourself but for all of us."

"It would be useless to provoke more bloodshed," sighed Lee.

For another hour he agonized over the decision, asking every general officer and staff member for their opinion. The majority agreed that an honorable surrender was the best available course. Finally he dictated a message to Grant.

General,

I request an interview at such time and place as you may designate, to discuss the terms of surrender of this army.

"I know Grant pretty well," said Longstreet, hoping to console his beloved commander-in-chief. "His terms would be what you would demand under the circumstances."

"I could not accept unconditional surrender."

"If he won't give you honorable terms, break it off, and tell him to do his damnedest."

Lee smiled bleakly and put a hand on Longstreet's shoulder. "My old warhorse," he murmured.

It did not take long for Grant to respond, indicating his willingness to meet with Lee anywhere, anytime. Followed by his staff, Lee rode down to Appomattox Court House. All along the way, Confederate soldiers found the strength to stand and cheer him as he rode by. Lee held onto his self-control by a mere thread.

One of his aides, Colonel Charles Marshall, rode ahead to find a suitable place for the meeting. He selected the house of Wilmer McLean. McLean was honored by Lee's presence, and showed the commander to the front parlor, where Lee sat at a small table by the south window. He placed his hat and gauntlets on the table. McLean admired his sword, noting that the weapon's handle appeared to be ivory, and was crowned with the head of a lion. The scabbard was blue steel, edged in gilt. Lee declined McLean's offer of something to drink and gazed pensively out the window at a group of ragged, gray warriors, lying or sitting on the grass in the shade of the locust trees.

Dalton whiled away the hours gazing at the countryside. For four years he had fought on the soil of the Old Dominion, from Manassas in the north—almost near enough to Washington D.C. to hear the church bells of the Federal capital ring—to Petersburg in the pine barrens south of Richmond. He had never taken the time or had the eye to appreciate Virginia's natural beauty. But now, as he awaited the inevitable end, he looked about him, aware that he would never see this land again. Already he knew that he would be leaving the South forever.

He studied the fields, scored by deep, red ravines, a nearby wooded ridge and beyond that a higher ridge with leaning fields at its base hacked out of the hardwood forests. Over yonder, where the pale-green willows marked its course, was the Appomattox River, hardly more than a narrow run at this point, for its headwaters lay amongst the steep, wood-cloaked knobs to the west. Beyond those knobs lay the Blue Ridge Mountains, and some few hundred miles west of them the mighty Mississippi. But it was the vast and largely uncharted frontier which lay west of the Father of Waters which intrigued him now.

"Are you going home to Alabama?" Margaret asked him, and he had a hunch she knew what he was thinking.

"I have nothing to go back to. And I have no desire to live in a conquered country."

"So what will you do?"

"I doubt if I would be welcome in the North," he said dryly. "So I guess that leaves the West."

"And what will you do out west?"

"Good Lord, I don't know. I'm not very good at anything but war." He thought, belatedly, that maybe she was trying to find out where she fit into the scheme of things, and realized that he hadn't made a very appealing case for her to accompany him. He wanted to come straight out and ask her to stay with him. But what did he have to offer? What kind of life would she be condemned to live as he drifted without purpose or prospects? "Look, ma'am—Margaret, I . . . "

She shook her head. "I know what you are about to say. But I'm not asking for assurances. If you wouldn't mind the company . . . "

"What about your home?"

"The Yankees will take it. We sold almost everything of

value during the war. With the field hands gone I could grow no money crops. I couldn't pay the taxes. They would just take it away from me, sooner or later. The house is gone now, the fields ruined. But if you don't want me . . . "

"No. I would like for you to come along."

She took his hand and her smile seemed to fill the void inside him.

"Yankees coming," murmured Muldoon.

"It's Grant," said Pease.

Dalton studied the Federal commander-in-chief with keen curiosity. Grant sat his horse well, a short, stocky figure in a thoroughly disreputable uniform. Here was a man who obviously put no stock in appearances. Except for the shoulder straps of a lieutenant general—rectangles of black velvet bearing three stars and bordered in gold— he might have been a private. A slouch hat was pulled low over his eyes, and a "short six" cigar jutted from his teeth. He wore neither sword nor spurs. A dozen officers rode with him, all of them more resplendent than he in their dress uniforms. As Grant and his entourage entered the McLean house, Pease checked his stemwinder. It was one-thirty in the afternoon.

At precisely four o'clock, General Lee and his aides emerged. Pease was immediately on his feet.

"He's still wearing his sword," he observed.

"Grant let him keep it," guessed Dalton.

"I'm going to see if I can find out what the terms were."

Grant came out onto the porch as Lee rode across the yard, and raised a hand in farewell. Lee returned the gesture, and continued on to the Lynchburg road. His passage was marked by cheering throngs of Rebel soldiers.

Dalton watched thirty or forty Yankee officers, who seemed to appear out of nowhere, descend on McLean's house and begin to methodically loot it. Tables, chairs, and pictures were carried out as souvenirs. Some of the officers tried to force McLean to accept greenback dollars in payment. The Virginian threw the money on the ground.

A Federal lieutenant approached Dalton and his men.

"You boys will have to move on," he said curtly. "General Sheridan intends to make his headquarters here."

"Well," drawled Dalton, irritated by the man's peremptory manner, "we sure wouldn't want to inconvenience General Sheridan."

The lieutenant glowered, turned on his heel, and walked briskly away.

"How do you like that?" asked one of Dalton's men. "A Yankee throwing us off our own Southern ground."

"They've been doing it for months," said Muldoon sharply. "Have you just now noticed?"

Pease returned.

"This is the way it is, gents. Officers give their individual paroles not to take up arms against the United States again, and each company or regimental commander signs a similar parole for the men under his direct command. Officers may keep their sidearms. All muskets and rifles to be turned over. And those who own a horse or a mule can keep it. They said Grant wanted to make sure we could work our farms this spring." He smirked.

"That's a mighty big help for us infantry boys, ain't it," said one of the soldiers.

"Oh, and lest I forget, the Yankees are giving each of us three days' rations—fresh beef, salt, hardtack, coffee, and sugar."

The men stared in disbelief at one another.

"My Gawd," said one. "Is that what them bluebellies been eatin'? It's a blamed wonder they can even march, takin' in all that kind of food."

Pease took Dalton aside. "I suppose we had better give

up these horses, Jack. They've got the U.S. brand on them. I doubt they would pass for our plow horses."

"I'm not going to walk all the way to the Mississippi River," said Dalton.

"Lord knows what they would do to you if they caught you on one of these nags."

"I'll worry about that when the time comes." Dalton stuck out a hand and forced a smile which he hoped looked nonchalant. "Well, Clement, I guess this is the end of the road at last."

Pease shook the hand vigorously. "We gave it one hell of a try, Jack. No one can say otherwise."

"Yes, we gave the Yankees a run for their money."

"We came up a bit short, but there's no shame in that, is there?"

"None." Dalton turned away quickly, embarrassed by what looked like tears in Clement's eyes.

He went to Margaret and told her it was time to go.

"But I thought I heard the lieutenant say something about your signing a parole for your men."

"I'll leave that to the regimental commander. I don't want to stick around here any longer than I have to. But I must warn you, Margaret, unless you want to walk over the mountains, that we will have to take those horses yonder. They are the property of the United States Army."

"I'll leave that to you." She seemed unconcerned.

Dalton nodded. He said good-bye to each of his men in turn, and wished them luck. Far as he knew, they were all planning to return to Alabama. He was afraid they were not going to like what they found there. Things would not be at all the same as they had been before the war.

He and Margaret left Appomattox Court House going cross-country, avoiding the roads, steering clear of soldiers both blue and gray. The stillness of the afternoon took some getting used to—for the past week Dalton had heard almost continuous musket or cannon fire. But now he heard nary a shot. The wind sighed in the treetops. The creeks sang as they danced in their beds of stone. But something was missing. It took a while for Dalton to figure out what that something was. The birds. He did not see or hear a single bird. The war had driven them all away. He wondered if they would ever come back.

6

The war was over for the Army of Northern Virginia and the Army of the Potomac. But there were other armies. Dalton knew there were at least ten thousand Yankees in the Shenandoah Valley and it was entirely possible that they would shoot first and ask questions later. Staying out of sight wasn't too difficult while they were in the mountains, but the Shenandoah was very open terrain with a plethora of towns, and he didn't give much for their chances of remaining undetected in the valley.

For this reason he stopped at the first farm they came to out of the mountains, and hoped that the occupants would react positively to butternut-gray. He was in luck. The farmer and his wife were diehard Confederates. Their two sons had perished for the Cause, and they hated the Yankees with a fierce passion. Not too many months ago Phil Sheridan and his bluecoat plunderers had laid waste to the Shenandoah. This was sound military strategy—the valley was the Confederacy's breadbasket, the source of most of Lee's supplies. But the farmer and his wife didn't give a hoot for military strategy. The Yankees had burned their crops and stolen every last pig and chicken, and it was a wonder they hadn't made off with the milch cow. Would have, if the durned critter hadn't broke out of its pen and wandered down to the creek to stand in the water and cool itself.

Dalton and Margaret were treated like visiting royalty. The farmer was eager for news of the war, and Dalton hated to be the one to tell him that Lee had surrendered four days ago. The news seemed to suck all the wind of the plowpusher's lungs.

They were fed and urged to stay the night, but Dalton didn't want to put the couple at risk. No telling what the Yankees would do if they found those horses with the U.S. brand in the farmer's barn. So they moved on—but not before the farmer gave Dalton some of his oldest son's clothes.

"He was about your size," said the farmer wistfully. "Tall, strapping young feller. Good-looking cuss, too. Ask any of the young girls hereabouts. They'd tell you. There are still plenty of Yankees out there itching to pull the trigger at one of them uniforms like you got on. So take these clothes and don't make a big issue out of it."

They made several more miles before nightfall. It was slow going. Dalton moved cautiously, trying to stick to the woods, or down in the creases between the rolling amber hills. That evening they made their camp by a creek, in a stand of willows and elms, not risking a fire, though the night promised to be a cool one, eating the cornbread and smoked meat the farmer's wife had pressed upon them. They took turns going down to the creek to bathe, and when he was done Dalton put on the civilian clothes— trousers of heavy, durable stroud, a linsey-woolsey shirt, an old felt hat. It felt strange to be out of uniform. Margaret stared at him, making him feel even more self-conscious, when he returned to camp.

"Good fit," she said.

"A dead man's clothes and a Yankee horse," said Dalton, with a rueful smile. "Some new beginning."

"It will get better."

"You're quite a woman, Margaret Talcott."

"Aren't you lucky?"

He laughed. It sounded strange to his ears, and he wondered how long it had been since he had laughed. "I believe so." He proceeded to roll the uniform around his sword.

"Are you going to keep those things?" she asked.

"I thought about wrapping them around a rock and dropping them into a creek. But I couldn't bring myself to do it. I know it might be dangerous keeping them, and I'll get rid of them if you say the word."

"No. Keep them if that's what you want to do."

Dalton unrolled his blanket. A Yankee blanket, blue wool with two broad black stripes at either end. His thoughts dwelled for a moment on the previous owner— another dead man, perhaps with a family like that farmer and his wife, with a trunk full of a lost son's clothes.

These grim reflections gave way to shock as he watched Margaret spread her blanket beside his. On previous nights she had slept a respectable distance away. But this time she lay down very close, with her back to him, hands beneath her head.

"Going to be cold tonight," she said.

Of course, it had been cold the night before, and the one before that, up in the Blue Ridge, but Dalton saw no point in bringing this to her attention.

"Just hold me, if you don't mind," she added, in a small voice.

Dalton didn't mind at all. He nervously draped one brawny arm over her. Nestling against him, she was soon sound asleep. But Dalton didn't care to sleep. He lay there and gazed up at the stars glittering like flecks of frost in the sky, and marvelled at the soft warmth and sweet, womanly smell of her.

They made it across the Shenandoah without mishap, crossing the path of a single Federal patrol, with no harm done. Plunging into the rugged wilderness of West Virginia, Dalton breathed a little easier. Through the Allegheny Mountains, across the Tygart Valley, until they struck the Little Kanawha River and followed it west by north towards Parkersburg. This was a country, rugged and beautiful, of small, remote farms and a scattering of isolated villages. The war had never visited here.

It was at a stage stop near Glenville that they learned of the assassination of Abraham Lincoln.

A woman named Crenshaw ran the place, with the help of her two sons, ages fourteen and twelve. The stages ran every other day between Parkersburg and points east, but Mrs. Crenshaw seldom had women to talk to, and was exceedingly glad to have the opportunity with Margaret. They hit it off immediately. She invited Dalton and Margaret to stay over for the night, and brushed aside Dalton's admission that they had no money with which to pay. Noting the brands on her guests' horses, she discreetly asked no questions.

The next morning, early, while Dalton and Margaret and the Crenshaws were just sitting down to breakfast, the westbound coach rolled in, and the reinsman gave them the news. The president had been shot down in cold blood by an actor named John Wilkes Booth. Lincoln had been attending a play at Ford's Theater, and Booth, a Southern sympathizer, had slipped unnoticed into the president's box and shot Lincoln in the back of the head with a derringer. The driver produced newspapers, bound for Parkersburg, which corroborated his story.

The newspapers gave all the lurid details. After shoot-

ing the president, Booth had leapt from the box onto the
stage below, catching the spur of his boot in the American
flag which draped the balcony, and falling poorly as a
result, snapping the bone in his leg. Brandishing a knife,
Booth had shouted "Sic semper tyrannis!" and fled out
the back way.

Lincoln was taken across the street from the theater
into a private home where, despite the efforts of several
distinguished physicians, he passed away the following
morning, April 15, having never regained consciousness.

Apparently, Booth was only part of a conspiracy to
deal the government of the United States a mortal blow.
At almost the very moment that Booth pulled the trigger
on Lincoln, an unidentified assailant, armed with a gun
and a knife, gained entrance into the residence of William
Seward, the Secretary of State. Seward had recently
injured himself in a carriage accident, and was bedridden.
The would-be assassin was stopped at the Secretary of
State's bedroom door by Frederick, Seward's son, but
fought his way into the bedroom, despite the fact that his
gun, fortunately for Frederick, missed fire. Seward was
wounded in the neck and head by the knife-wielding
assailant, and would have been killed but for the neck
and jaw braces which he was wearing as a consequence of
his previous mishap. His assailant fled in the night,
shouting, "I am mad! I am mad!" as he bounded down
the stairs and out the door.

There were rumors to the effect that the sinister plot
had meant to include a third victim in the person of
Andrew Johnson, the vice president. Some surmised
that the Confederacy was behind the plot. Dalton considered that to be a patently absurd notion. The government
of the Confederate States of America was populated by
honorable gentlemen who would not have stooped to
such an act. Besides, they were scattered to the four

winds, with President Jefferson Davis fleeing to points south with the meager Treasury, one step ahead of pursuing Federals.

As they were preparing to leave the stage station, Mrs. Crenshaw took Dalton discreetly aside.

"I think you would be better off without those horses," she said.

"How do you mean?"

"Booth and his accomplices are still at large. The assassination of President Lincoln will have every Federal soldier seeking vengeance. Not to mention a great many Northern civilians. There will be a manhunt unlike any this country has ever seen, and the repercussions will be terrible to behold."

"I hardly think Margaret and I will be mistaken for Booth, ma'am."

"That won't matter. Any suspicious persons will be harshly dealt with, I fear."

"Do I strike you as a suspicious person, Mrs. Crenshaw?"

She smiled. "Let me say first that I have not taken sides in this terrible war. My husband is fighting for the Union, but he left me long before he enlisted. To answer your question, those horses make you suspicious."

"What do you suggest?"

"Take the stage."

"We have no money."

"I will pay you, greenback dollars, for the horse."

"Why would you want to do that?"

"Because you and Margaret strike me as good, decent people who are only trying to escape this madness. I would like to help, and I happen to be in a position where I can do so. I will tell the Federals I found these horses as strays. There won't be any questions asked of me."

Dalton shook his head. "I can't accept your charity."

"Don't let your pride defeat you, Mr. Dalton," she said sternly. "Think about what is best for Margaret. I can tell that you care a great deal for her."

Dalton felt his cheeks burn. "Is it that obvious?"

"That you are in love? Of course."

"We'll leave the horses with you."

"I can only afford to give you about sixty dollars for the pair."

"I will repay you. Someday."

"Don't worry about that."

"I will worry, until the debt is paid."

7

At Parkersburg they crossed the Ohio River on the ferry, and booked passage north by stagecoach to Columbus, where Dalton thought they could catch a train west across Ohio, Indiana, and Illinois to Missouri. Traveling with them on the stage was a middle-aged and well-to-do couple as well as a man named Zebulon Bigelow, who identified himself as a correspondent for the *Baltimore Sun*.

Bigelow was a stocky, ebullient, good-natured fellow, the kind of man who puts you instantly at ease. This worked to his immense advantage, for people were inclined to drop their guard and say things they would not otherwise have said in any other reporter's presence. Having commanded men in battle, Dalton was an excellent judge of character, and he soon realized that the jovial, moon-faced correspondent with the flamboyant side whiskers and a fondness for expensive cigars had a keen wit and an incisive mind.

"I was on my way home from a long and strenuous stint with Sherman on his march to the sea when I was informed of Lincoln's death," explained Bigelow, who didn't seem to be entirely content unless he was talking.

"They are taking him back to Springfield by special train, and I have been assigned to cover the journey for my newspaper. I think I will call it the Black Pageant. Has a nice ring to it, don't you think?"

"You ought not to make light of it," protested the thin, pale, ascetic-looking man, clad in fine, black broadcloth, who sat across from Bigelow and Dalton, wedged between his wife and Margaret. "The president's murder at the hand of that damned secessionist is a catastrophe for the North."

"As well as for the South," murmured Bigelow. "I don't believe I caught your name, sir."

"Caulfield. Elijah Caulfield. This is my wife, Hannah. We are returning home to Cleveland. We have been this past fortnight at Shawnee Springs."

"Oh? Partaking of the cure?"

"The mineral baths are of some benefit to Hannah. She suffers from severe rheumatism. And we would appreciate your disposing of that cigar."

"Certainly." With reluctance, Bigelow pitched the long nine he had just fired up out the window of the stagecoach. "How fortunate for you, Mr. Caulfield, that you are able to vacation at Shawnee Springs in this day and time."

Caulfield's flinty eyes narrowed with suspicion. "I don't know that I like your tone, sir."

Dalton suppressed a smile. He had a hunch Bigelow was feeling a little vindictive for having been obliged to discard one of his expensive stogies.

"Just an observation," said Bigelow, smooth as silk. "That is, after all, what I am paid to do. Observe, and report what I see."

"I will have you know," said Caulfield, waxing indignant, "that I was not on vacation, as you call it. I have labored diligently in the service of my country since the war broke out. I was conducting business while my wife recuperated, as I have done every day of every week, with the exception of the Sabbath, of course, since those damned secessionists fired on our flag at Fort Sumter."

Bigelow was screening every word Caulfield said to hook onto some subject with which to nettle the man. "There are some who say that Lincoln bamboozled the Confederates into firing that first shot, just so he would not have to take the blame for starting the war."

"Outrageous!" exclaimed Caulfield, with some color in his cheeks now. "To speak with such rank disrespect about our martyred president! You should be ashamed, sir! Ashamed!"

"No disrespect intended. In fact, I thought it was admirably clever of him, at the time."

"Just the kind of talk I would expect from a Baltimore man."

"I'm not sure I know what you mean," said Bigelow, with steel behind his smile now. "Please be so kind as to clarify that last remark."

Mrs. Caulfield put a restraining hand on her husband's arm. "Don't, Elijah. It isn't good for a man your age to become so agitated."

"Agitated? Damn right I'm agitated. I will tell you exactly what I mean, sir. I mean that Baltimore has always been a hotbed of damned secessionists. I recall there was a plot back in the early days of the war to kill the president as he was passing through Baltimore, on his way to Washington to take up his duties as our chief magistrate."

"Ah. You refer to the Plug Uglies. Yes, I remember that. I remember the president slipped through Baltimore ahead of schedule, disguised as an old woman."

Caulfield was bordering on apoplexy. "That is traitorous talk." He turned to Dalton. "Don't you agree, sir?"

Dalton smiled. "I'm really not the one to ask about that."

"Nonsense," said Bigelow. "I am a devoted Unionist. The Southern states had no right to secede. Their argument—that since the states voluntarily agreed to enter into the compact which formed this great nation they therefore reserved the right to withdraw from it at their whim—was utterly specious. That is akin to saying that if I entered into a contract with you, sir, to provide me with a thousand rifles, that I would be within my rights to back out of the deal whenever it suited me. You would, I am sure, agree that this is nonsense."

"Certainly. But . . . how did you know . . . "

"That you are engaged in the business of manufacturing repeating rifles, and are under lucrative contract to provide that product to the United States Army?" Bigelow wore a sly smile. "I knew who you were the moment you identified yourself, Mr. Caulfield. You are quite right to be proud of your labors in the service of your country. Your repeating rifles contributed substantially to turning the tide of the war."

Dalton took a strong and instant dislike to Elijah Caulfield. He had seen too many of his men fall before the new Yankee repeaters to do otherwise.

"I wonder," mused Bigelow, cupping chin in hand and tapping the side of his nose with a forefinger, "what will you do now that the war is concluded? Will your profits suffer, Mr. Caulfield?"

"Not at all," said Caulfield. "Now that the damned secessionists have been put in their place, we can turn our attention once more to the frontier."

"Oh, you mean the Indians."

"Precisely. Our settlers out west have been catching hell from those damned heathens these past four years, because we could not spare enough troops from the eastern campaigns to protect them."

"I suppose that means I will be heading west eventually," sighed Bigelow—the melodramatic sigh of the long-suffering. "If we are to have an Indian War, my paper will insist that I cover it."

"They must be exterminated," said Caulfield, fervently. "And the repeating rifle will provide the means for doing so."

"They are fighting for their land," said Dalton. "Their way of life." He didn't know much about the Indian situation on the frontier, but he wanted to contradict Caulfield just for the hell of it.

Bigelow and the Caulfields stared at him for a moment, surprised by his unexpected participation in the conversation.

"So they say." Bigelow nodded. "The same argument the South used, by the way."

Caulfield scoffed at the notion. "The Secesh were traitors, every last one of them."

Bigelow shrugged, and fired a sly, sidelong glance at Dalton, and Dalton had a strong feeling suddenly that somehow the correspondent knew he had recently worn butternut-gray. It wasn't possible, of course—Dalton's uniform and sword were wrapped tightly in his blanket roll, riding now on the top rack of the stagecoach. Still, Bigelow's knowing glance seemed to say *He is calling you a traitor. What are you going to do about it?* Dalton decided to steer the conversation down another path.

"You said Lincoln's murder was a catastrophe for the South. How is that?"

"Despite what the esteemed Mr. Caulfield thinks," said Bigelow, "I am an ardent admirer of Abe Lincoln. I don't know that any other man could have steered the Union safely through this extraordinary crisis. He was strong-minded, yet humble and compassionate. He was prepared to demonstrate that compassion in his dealing with a vanquished South. Case in point, his Ten Percent Plan."

Bigelow raised bushy eyebrows in a silent query. Dalton shook his head. He had never heard of any such plan.

"This is the way it would work," explained the correspondent. "As soon as ten percent of the population of a seceded state swore allegiance to the Union, that state would be admitted back into the fold."

"Pure poppycock," opined Caulfield. "I think we should make the South pay, and pay dearly, before accepting them back into the Union."

"You are in complete accord with the Radical Republicans, I take it," murmured Bigelow. He turned to Dalton. "The Radical Republicans control Congress. They didn't, though, until the Southern states seceded, taking all their Democratic congressmen with them. The Radical Republicans want to punish the South. In addition, they plan to secure their hold on the reins of government. Before the war, the Democrats ran things. As you may know, when the Southern representatives left Congress in sixty-one, they left the Republicans in charge, the first time in our history. The Republicans are in no hurry to give the Southern states their rights and privileges back. In so doing, they would pave the way for the Democrats to achieve another majority in both House and Senate. Abe Lincoln alone stood between them and the Southern states. His only concern was to heal the wounds of civil war as speedily as possible. But the Radical Republicans passionately opposed his Ten Percent Plan, as well as his ideas regarding complete amnesty for secessionist leaders."

"Hang 'em," growled Caulfield. "Hang 'em all and good riddance."

Bigelow chuckled. "You would treat them like criminals. Lincoln treated them like wayward children."

"So what happens now?" asked Dalton. "Now that

Lincoln is dead, do these Radical Republicans get their way?"

"That depends entirely on how strong-willed and independently minded Andrew Johnson turns out to be." Bigelow sounded dubious. "Few know much about his politics. He was chosen as Lincoln's running mate in sixty-four because of strong opposition to Hannibal Hamlin. Let me just say that I would not want to be a Southerner in these next several years. I suspect the Radical Republicans will enfranchise the freed slaves, who, of course, will be expected to show the proper gratitude and vote Republican. At the same time, the Southern leaders—almost all of whom are Democrats—will be disenfranchised."

Dalton glanced across the coach at Margaret. He wasn't sure if he understood everything Bigelow was saying, but it didn't sound good for the South. His thoughts turned to the survivors of his company, by now paroled and on their way home to Alabama. Sounded like they would find many changes wrought when they got there, and not all for the good.

The following day they reached Columbus. Bigelow volunteered to escort them to the train station, as he perceived that the hustle and bustle of this strange city made Dalton and Margaret a bit ill-at-ease. The correspondent paused on the way to purchase a local newspaper from a boy on a street corner. He slapped the paper and excitedly showed Dalton and Margaret the front page.

"Lincoln's body has left Washington on a funeral train bound for Springfield," he said. "Three hundred assorted dignitaries aboard. It has passed through Baltimore and Harrisburg already. There were riots in Philadelphia, spectators crushed to death as a line of mourners three miles long waited to view the body. Three hundred thousand people! Next came New York. A funeral procession up Broadway, over to Fifth Avenue, on to Thirty-fourth Street, thence to Ninth Avenue and the depot—a procession four hours long! They say that New York may be the last open-coffin procession. It seems the poor president's jaw has fallen, and his face turned black."

"How awful," said Margaret.

"Indeed," Bigelow nodded. "A rather macabre way to lay a man to rest, when you think on it—a seventeen-hundred-mile excursion, with a funeral at every whistle stop. Oh well. Let's see—Buffalo, then Cleveland, then finally Columbus. Two days, if the schedule printed here remains accurate. I will have to work myself aboard that train somehow, accompany it on to Cincinnati, Indianapolis, Chicago." Bigelow sighed. "Much weeping and sackcloth. I don't doubt that I will be tremendously relieved when they put the poor man in his grave and Abe Lincoln can finally rest in peace. Of course, I shall have to describe every gory detail for the Baltimore reading public. Hearses pulled by a team of six black horses, accompanied by maidens in white, reminiscent of those who led fallen Viking warriors to Valhalla. I shall say, 'Hushed is the city. Hung be the sky in black. Let the streets be still. Let the winds be lulled. Let the sun be covered up. The bells—toll them. The guns—let their melancholy boom roll out.'" Bigelow seemed to be transported by his own eloquence. He shook himself out of it and noticed that Dalton was staring at him. "Too ornate, do you think?"

Arriving at the train depot, they could see that preparations were already being made—barricades erected, black bunting and American flags secured to every pillar and facade. Bigelow helped them secure passage on the afternoon train, which passed through Cincinnati and Vincennes on the way to the Mississippi, and terminated at St. Louis. When they were all set, Bigelow took his leave, expressing dismay at the task of finding a hotel room, shaking Dalton's hand and taking Margaret's with a deft, Continental bow.

"I wish you both the very best in your new beginning," he said.

"Thank you for all that you have done," said Margaret.

"The pleasure was entirely mine, ma'am." Turning to go, he thought of something, giving Dalton a sly wink. "For what it's worth, sir, I don't consider you a traitor. But take care. Others do."

With that he was gone.

8

With every mile the train rolled and racketed west, a little more of the tension pent up inside Dalton escaped. He was putting the war behind him, and a great weight seemed to be lifted off his shoulders. The Confederacy was dead, but he had survived, and, best of all, Margaret was with him. For the first time in four years he allowed himself to consider the future. He had very little money in his pocket. He had no idea what to expect on the frontier. Nor did he have a clue what he would do to make a living.

His father had been a dirt-poor farmer, and when he died, a year before secession, Dalton had tried to keep the farm going for the sake of his ailing mother. She had passed away in '61, having lost the will to live after losing the man she had been married to for thirty years. The day Dalton buried her next to his father was the same day he walked off the farm and enlisted.

Volunteer companies were permitted to choose their own officers, and the men had chosen him as one of their sergeants, an honor which had come as a complete surprise to Dalton. He had risen to the rank of captain by virtue of battlefield promotions. War was hell, as Sherman had said, but Dalton had been good at it, and much preferred it to farming. Never again did he wish to touch another plow.

So what options were left open to him? Caulfield had mentioned Indian wars, but that was out of the question, too. Dalton would never fight under the Stars and Stripes. He was reconciled by now to the surrender, but not to repatriation. Pease had asked him why he had gone to war in the first place—now he remembered. Because there had been nothing else for him to do. He had not fought for the perpetuation of slavery, or some notion like states' rights, but he had become as passionate a foe of the Union as any firebrand secessionist. He did not love the South so much that he could not leave her, as he was doing now, without regret. But the Yankees were the enemy. They had killed his friends. They had tried to kill him. After four years of the horror and suffering and fear and violence of war he could not stop hating the enemy. Every time he saw the Stars and Stripes he tasted bile. Maybe time would change that.

He saw the flag quite often as the train took them across Ohio and Indiana and Illinois. The flag was everywhere. Bands were playing. People clogged the streets of every town in celebration. A newspaper discarded by another passenger informed him of the surrender of Joe Johnston's army. Just as well, he mused, that he had not escaped Grant's trap and joined Johnston in the Carolinas. The war was truly over now, and the North was celebrating, and not even the death of their beloved president could prevent them from savoring the triumph.

He learned, too, somewhere in Illinois, eavesdropping on the conversation of two men on a bench across the aisle, that John Wilkes Booth had been cornered and killed. Dalton shook his head. Sheer madness, this assassination. He was glad Booth had been brought down, having no sympathy for cowards who shot their victims in the back. Worse, Booth had thought he was striking a blow for the Confederacy, when in fact he had dealt the South a severe blow instead. Yankee retaliation would be harsh.

Yet, in spite of the fact that he did not know what he would do out west, Dalton experienced a strange contentment as he sat on the hard bench in the passenger car and watched the fertile fields and wooded knolls of Illinois pass by, with Margaret beside him. Sometimes she slept with her head on his shoulder and the faint fragrance of flowers from her chestnut-brown hair filled his nostrils, and he knew she was the reason the uncertainty of tomorrow did not concern him overmuch. Already, in only a fortnight, they had been through so much together, and there was a conviction growing within him that as long as they were together all would be well. She was his deliverance, and the only thing he feared was losing her.

A ferry took them across the mighty Mississippi to the St. Louis docks, but they did not linger in the bustling city, catching a ride on a freight wagon to Independence. The muleskinner was a salty, sunwhacked character who called himself Three Finger Smith.

"Used to, I fancied myself a knife fighter on a par with Bowie," said the garrulous freighter. "Then I got a bit careless—and I reckon I was a little drunk, too, come to think on it—and I cut off these here two fingers on my right hand. Well, my knife fightin' days were purty much a fond memory after that. But I ain't had no trouble to speak of since. It's my reputation, y'see. A reputation will take you a fur piece in this country, mister. Why, you could be a lily-livered coward and folks would cross a muddy street to get out of your way, if you had a reputation."

"I'll remember that," said Dalton.

"Where you folks headed?"

"We heard that wagon trains bound for the mountains leave out of Independence."

Three Finger nodded. "That they do. Me, I'm fixin' to join up with an outfit carrying goods to Taos by way of the Cimarron Cutoff. You might find some folks headed on up the Oregon or Bozeman Trails. Not so many nowadays as a few years ago, on account of the Injuns have been actin' up lately." He gave Dalton a sidelong once-over. "But you ain't got a horse or wagon, pilgrim. You aimin' to walk two thousand miles to the Shining Mountains, are you?"

"If we have to."

"Don't rightly know that you'll find a wagonmaster willin' to take you on. Might sign you on as a scout if you had a good pony and could read sign and knew the plains like the back of your hand. Or a hunter, but there again you'd have to have yourself a pony and a rifle. You ain't got a rifle, fur as I can tell."

"No," said Dalton. "Just this." He showed Three Finger the Whitney.

The muleskinner eyed the revolver askance. "Hell, pilgrim, what you aimin' to kill with that peashooter? Might do back east. But out here we grow things bigger and meaner. Shoot, I've seen jackrabbits big as dogs you couldn't drop with that." Three Finger tugged a gun that was longer than his forearm out of his belt. "Now this is the size charcoal burner you'll want to own. Walker Colt, .45 caliber. You can shoot through brick walls with this feller. Drop a bull buffalo dead in his tracks at a hunnerd yards."

"Well," said Dalton, "maybe if I wave this peashooter at it, it will die laughing."

Three Finger guffawed. "I like you, pilgrim. Tell you what. I could use some company on the Taos trail. Interested?"

"Might be."

"Thing is, it ain't no place for a woman. No offense, ma'am, but them Comanch' will play hell with us. You can bank on it. And then there's snakes and scorpions and dust storms and wild-eyed rivers and such to contend with."

"We travel together," said Dalton.

"You two been married long?"

Dalton smiled at Margaret. "Not long."

She smiled back.

"What army was you with?" asked Three Finger.

Dalton's dark eyes narrowed. "What makes you think I was with any army?"

"You got the war written all over you, pilgrim. Now don't go gettin' your hackles up. I never wanted anything to do with that blame fool war, myself. I ain't for the North or the South. I'm just naturally curious. Gets me into trouble ever' now and then."

"The Army of Northern Virginia," said Dalton. First Bigelow, now Three Finger Smith. Seemed like he couldn't pull the wool over anybody's eyes. They took one look at him and knew him for a Rebel. "Might as well wear my uniform," he said to Margaret.

"Better not," advised Three Finger. "It's been a nasty business, this war, here in Missouri. You got folks like Quantrill and Anderson and the Redlegs from over Kansas way. They don't play by the rules. What I hear, the war's over back east. Ain't the case here. Not by a long shot. Those Confederate partisans have been playing hell, and most of 'em ain't surrendered yet. Their favorite tactic is to slip down out of the hills and hit the Yanks when they least expect it. Makes the bluecoats right onry. Nossir, don't you go wearin' that uniform of yours if you want to get out of Missouri alive."

Franklin was the first town they came to which had a distinctly frontier flavor to it. Wide, dusty, rutted streets, false front buildings of weathered clapboard, an aura of impermanence, as though everything that was here could be gone tomorrow. The community, three days' travel west of St. Louis, had been the point of rendezvous for outfits destined for one of the trails west. So it was that many of the people on its streets and sidewalks, its stores and saloons, were on their way somewhere else.

Dalton was quick to notice that there were a lot of Yankee soldiers in town. They seemed to be everywhere, mostly in twos and threes.

"Sumpin's happened," opined a solemn Three Finger Smith. He stopped the wagon in front of a mercantile. "The feller what runs this place is an amigo of mine. I reckon all these bluecoats are here on account of some trouble with the Rebel raiders. I'll find out for sure, though." He winked at Dalton. "Could be Injuns. If it is, it'll be my concern. If it's Rebels, it'll be yours. Keep an eye on my possibles while I'm gone."

He disappeared inside the mercantile, leaving Dalton and Margaret on the wagon seat. A pair of young soldiers sauntered by on the boardwalk, and gave them a long, speculative look in passing.

"I don't like this," said Margaret, and Dalton felt an involuntary shudder wrack her body. He couldn't blame her. After what had happened with the cavalrymen at her house, she had ample reason for reacting negatively to the blue uniforms.

"Don't worry," he said, fighting the sensation of being in a trap. "As soon as Smith comes back, we'll get off the street." His gaze swept the buildings along the main thoroughfare of Franklin. "There's a hotel. We'll get a room."

"But we can't afford that."

"It's been a long and difficult trip from Virginia, Maggie. We could both stand a decent meal and a good night's sleep in a comfortable bed."

Her embarrassed smile made him realize what he had said, and he blushed, and hoped his beard concealed the fact.

"I mean, we'll get two rooms, of course. . . . "

"But wouldn't that appear a bit out of the ordinary? For a married couple to get separate hotel rooms?"

"I didn't mean to . . . well, it just seemed better, under the circumstances, to tell Smith . . . "

"For heaven's sakes, don't apologize," she said. "Actually, I kind of like the idea." Now it was her turn to blush. "Oh, I'm sorry! I'm not usually so . . . so bold."

"Maggie, I . . . "

She shook her head. "I wasn't fishing for a proposal. We've only known each other a couple of weeks."

"Even so," said Dalton, "we've been through a lot together in that little time." He looked around and smiled. "This is a funny place for it, in a wagon in the middle of the street in Franklin, Missouri—but, what the hell. Will you marry me?"

"Yes. I knew we would be husband and wife the moment I first saw you."

Dalton experienced a rare contentment at that moment.

Three Finger Smith returned. "It's Rebels they're after. They bushwhacked a bluecoat supply train a few miles from here. Mebbe you folks ought to go on to Independence with me. That's where my outfit is going to rendezvous."

Dalton shook his head. "No, but thanks, all the same. My wife is tired. We'll rest up here for a day or two."

"Pilgrim, you watch out for these bluecoats. They're mad as hornets."

Dalton climbed down out of the wagon. "The war is over for me," he said. "I've got something to live for now."

"Huh?" Three Finger scratched his grizzled jaw.

"Nothing." Dalton helped Margaret down, retrieved their blanket rolls from beneath the wagon seat. "Good luck to you, Mr. Smith."

"And to you folks." Three Finger got back aboard and stirred up the mule team.

Dalton and Margaret crossed the street to the hotel, arm in arm.

"Perhaps we could find a preacher," she said, "and save the cost of one room."

His expression made her laugh. Dalton was so disconcerted that all he could do was gape at her. So he wasn't paying attention as they neared the open doors to the hotel lobby, and collided with a soldier coming out of the establishment. The collision knocked the blanket rolls from under Dalton's arm.

Mumbling an apology, the soldier picked up the blankets. As he did, the string holding Dalton's blanket roll together gave way. Dalton's sword and uniform fell out at the soldier's feet.

The soldier stared at the butternut-gray uniform.

"I can explain," said Dalton.

But as the soldier looked up at him with hot, angry eyes, Dalton could see that no explanation would suffice.

He was looking into the eyes of the enemy.

"Damn Rebel," muttered the soldier, backing up, and his hand dropped to the flap of his side holster.

9

"No," said Dalton, holding his arms out away from his sides. "The war is over."

But the soldier didn't hear him. He had the flap open and was tugging his pistol out of the holster, still backing up. As far as he was concerned, Dalton was a rattlesnake. You didn't talk to a rattlesnake. You didn't try to reason with it. You killed it. The only good rattlesnake was a dead one. The same applied to Rebels.

Dalton could see there would be no reasoning with this man. Still, he desperately wanted to avoid any shooting. For one thing, this was no place for fighting a battle, in a town crawling with trigger-happy bluecoats. For another, there was Margaret to consider. She might get caught in the line of fire. . . .

Even as he thought it, the unthinkable happened.

"Look out!" cried Margaret. She could see it as clearly as Dalton—the soldier was going to draw his pistol and shoot and only one thing would prevent him: Dalton had to shoot first. But Dalton wasn't going for the Whitney in his belt. No, he was just standing there with his arms out, as though he were daring the soldier to shoot him.

She lunged, pushing Dalton as the soldier's Schofield revolver spat flame.

Dalton watched in horror as the impact of the bullet propelled Margaret, falling, into him. The soldier fired a second time—Dalton assumed at him—but the second bullet struck her, too, high in the shoulder. Sagging in his arms, she made a small, pitiful sound. He laid her down on the blood-splattered boardwalk, paying the threat of the soldier's Schofield no heed, trying to deny what his own eyes were seeing as he stared at the dark stain of blood on her dress. Her eyes were closed, and he was afraid—very afraid—that they would never open again.

Finally, belatedly heeding the frantic scream of his well-developed survival instinct, he looked around at the soldier. The soldier was gaping at Margaret, realizing what he had done. For an instant he forgot all about killing Dalton. But when he saw the look in Dalton's eyes he remembered.

"You bastard," breathed Dalton.

Rising, he swept the Whitney from his belt, his eyes blazing with a murderous rage.

The soldier took another step back as he fired, jarring his gun arm against the wall of the hotel, and the bullet made an ugly, cracking sound as it missed Dalton by scant inches. Dalton didn't even flinch. He aimed the Whitney and squeezed the trigger. He had been under fire too many times to be unnerved by the experience. The bullet made a neat, blue hole in the soldier's forehead, then blew the back of his skull off, splattering blood and brains all over the wall. The soldier's corpse hit the boardwalk so hard it bounced.

Dalton whirled at the sound of footsteps. Another soldier appeared in the hotel doorway. He looked at Margaret, at the dead bluecoat, then at Dalton—and his eyes got wide as a prospector's pan. He threw his hands out in front of him, as though trying to fend Dalton off.

"Don't shoot!" he shrieked, his voice cracking. "I'm not—"

The Whitney spoke, and the bullet struck the soldier squarely in the chest, and he sprawled backwards on the threadbare carpet covering the lobby floor. His heels beat a quick tattoo and then he was gone.

Dalton knew what the man had been trying to say— that he wasn't armed.

"Too damned bad," muttered Dalton, without a twinge of remorse.

Turning, he coldly surveyed the street. Civilians and soldiers alike were running—the civilians scattering, the bluecoats converging on the hotel, charging to the sound of battle. There were seven in the street, four coming from one direction, three from the other, and another running along the boardwalk, shooting as he ran. His bullets splintered the sign above the hotel doorway. Dalton shook his head, contemptuous. You didn't shoot and run at the same time. That was a waste of ammunition. Turning his body slightly to present the smallest possible target, like a duellist, he aimed the Whitney and fired. The bluecoat dove for cover. Dalton's bullet caught him in the thigh and knocked him down. The soldier crawled into an alley between the hotel and the adjacent building, grunting like a stuck pig, leaving his pistol on the boardwalk. Seeing this, Dalton forgot the man and turned his attention to the rest of the enemy.

The thought of getting away never occurred to him. His sole purpose in life now was to take as many bluecoats as he could with him down the road to Hell.

He had three bullets remaining in the Whitney—this was the kind of thing he never forgot, even in the heat of battle—and with Yankees closing in from all sides he knew he would not have time to reload. So he scooped up the Schofield of the first bluecoat he had killed, the bastard who'd shot Margaret, and began to blast away at the soldiers running in the street, firing the Schofield and the Whitney simultaneously. Four shoots up the street, and one of the soldiers went down, gut shot, while another was spun around as a bullet shattered the bones in his upper arm—he stumbled away, clutching at the wound, blood gushing through his fingers. The others scattered, seeking cover.

Dalton turned his attention to the other end of the street, just as a bullet smashed into an upright next to him, and another grooved the boardwalk near his foot. Unfazed, wreathed in gunsmoke, his eyes black and cold like the grave, Dalton thumbed the hammers back on the pistols and sent two more slugs chasing the bluecoats, who were already headed for cover. The Whitney was empty now; he drew a bead on a fleeing soldier with the Schofield. The man was trying to dodge into the mercantile store across and down the street, the same store Three Finger Smith had visited a few minutes ago, the store in front of which Margaret had said yes to his clumsy proposal of marriage.

Margaret . . .

Dalton's taut lips pulled back from clenched teeth in a snarl of pure hate. The soldier was running away. He was no threat to Dalton. But he wore the blue uniform—the uniform Dalton despised—and Dalton aimed and fired. The Schofield bucked in his hand. The bullet picked the soldier up off his feet and propelled him through the mercantile's plate glass window.

Suddenly the street was empty. The citizens of Franklin, Missouri, in the heart of Rebel guerrilla country, were accustomed to abrupt explosions of violence—they wasted no time in finding holes and crawling into them. The soldiers had vanished, too. But they would be back.

Dalton knew this, but he didn't care. In fact, he wanted them to come.

Discarding the Whitney, he tucked the Schofield under his belt. The latter had a bigger caliber and was very accurate. Dalton unbuckled the belt of the first man he had shot down, seeing that there was a cartridge pouch attached. Then he turned to Margaret again, forced himself to look at her, even though it nearly killed him to do it. He was shocked by the amount of blood, a pool of it appearing from beneath her. He knew she was dead, but made himself kneel and feel for a pulse in her throat. There was none. Eyes burning, he touched her lovely face, so composed and peaceful and pale in death. An anguished groan escaped him.

The bullet knocked him sideways, onto the boardwalk.

It felt like the cold steel of a bayonet rammed into his side. The report of a rifle echoed down the deathly still street. Dalton glimpsed a blue uniform at the mouth of an alley across the way—he raised the empty Schofield and the soldier ducked back down the alley. Three of his comrades-in-arms were dead, two wounded, and one, gut shot, was dying in the middle of the street, whimpering like a pup. The soldier didn't want to join them.

Lying on his side, Dalton reloaded the Schofield, fumbling with the cartridges. His first thought was that he would just wait here and let them come and kill him. At least that way he and Margaret would die together. Then he saw his uniform, there on the blanket, within reach, and he thought, *It isn't time to die yet. I haven't killed enough of them. I haven't made them pay the price. They didn't want the war to be over? That's fine with me. They don't know what war is—yet.*

He reached out, wincing, trying to ignore the pain, and gathered up the butternut-gray tunic, somewhat tattered and frayed. Then he willed himself to his feet, and once on his feet, willed himself to stay conscious, as the world began to spin madly, and the ground seemed to tilt sharply beneath him. Using the tunic as a compress against the bleeding hole in his side, he staggered to the alley running alongside the hotel. He didn't look back at Margaret. Couldn't bear to. It was hard, so hard, just to leave her. But he had to. He had a war to wage. And this war, unlike the one he had just finished, was personal.

Down the alley, in a stumbling run, weaving like a drunken man. Someone appeared at the back door of the hotel—a civilian, who jumped back inside as Dalton swung the Schofield in his direction. Across a lot filled with trash and clumps of dusty buffalo grass. Down another alley. From the main street came a smattering of gunshots. Dalton smiled grimly. What did they think they were shooting at? He had them spooked.

On the next street over he went to the first horse, a coyote dun, tethered to a hitching pole in front of a dentist's office. There were a few people on the street, standing around, wondering what the gunplay signified, but when they saw Dalton they vanished like ghosts. No one disputed him on the subject of the horse. He hauled himself into the saddle, a supreme effort of will, and left Franklin at a hard gallop, bent forward with his pain-twisted face buried in the horse's mane, heading west onto the prairie.

10

When Captain Ben Wettermark arrived in Franklin at the head of his trail-weary patrol, he found an armed guard on the road at the edge of town, and from these two men learned three things.

One was that the town was under martial law, by the order of Colonel Lewis, the regimental commanding officer. Second, a Rebel partisan had killed four men and wounded two others only a few hours ago. And third, that Colonel Lewis had informed all pickets that he wanted to see Wettermark as soon as the captain arrived.

Wettermark heaved a weary sigh. He was a slender young man, in his mid-twenties, of medium build, but his size was deceptive—physically he was stronger and more resilient than many a larger man. Having just led his troopers on a fruitless hundred-mile search for the elusive Confederate guerrillas who had recently ambushed an army supply train, he had been looking forward to a decent meal, a hot bath, and a good night's sleep. Somehow he knew now that he would have none of these things.

"Where is the colonel?" he asked one of the sentries.

"Down at the livery, I think, sir. That's where they got the woman laid out."

"Woman? What woman?"

"The one that got killed in the fight with that Rebel."

Wettermark was mystified, but decided it would be a waste of time to question the sentry further. Better to get all the details from Colonel Lewis, straight from the horse's mouth. Wettermark smiled. Or, more precisely, the horse's ass.

With a tired gesture he put the bedraggled, dusty column into motion. He could tell something had happened here. The town was very subdued. The streets were virtually empty, but for the grim-faced, fully armed soldiers.

Arriving at the livery, he told his lieutenant to take charge of the men. As he dismounted, Colonel Lewis appeared out of the dark, cool interior of the livery. Wettermark saluted briskly, but Lewis was looking past him, at the sorry state of the men and horses in the column moving on down the street.

"I take it you failed in your mission, Captain," said Lewis sourly.

Wettermark grimaced at the bad taste in his mouth. He very much wanted to tell Lewis that he had sent them on a fool's errand; that they'd had a snowball's chance in perdition of ever finding the partisans in the first place, and in the second place they probably would have been roundly whipped if they *had* managed to catch up with the Rebels. But Wettermark was a disciplined man who just tried to do his job as best he could and stay out of trouble, so he didn't speak his mind.

"Yes, sir," he replied, matter-of-factly.

Lewis gave him a look of disapproval, as though he expected at least a glimmer of remorse from Wettermark.

"Follow me, Captain."

Lewis turned on his heel and entered the livery. In his

wake, Wettermark swept the sweat-stained campaign hat from his head and ran gloved fingers through his tousled, yellow hair, relieved to be in the shade.

Just inside the livery, in the carriageway, a coffin lay across a pair of wooden sawhorses. At the other end of the carriageway, where another pair of big doors were open to a wagonyard, the blacksmith was sawing on wood with which to finish the coffin's lid.

The woman in the coffin, thought Wettermark, was strikingly pretty, even in death. Young, too, cut down in the prime of life. Wettermark shook his head sadly.

"Who is she, Colonel?"

"I don't give a damn who she is," said Lewis. "But I want the man she was with. The bastard killed four of my men, and wounded two others."

"One man did all that?"

Lewis gave him a dark look. "Yes. One man. And this whore."

Wettermark bit down hard on a sharp rebuke welling up inside him. Lewis was a crude, inconsiderate, and callous man. Not a soldier in the regiment liked him. The first rule for any commander was to take care of his soldiers. But Lewis didn't give a damn about his men. His commission was a political thing—he had no prior military experience. Now that the war was over, he would try to palm himself off as a military hero while seeking political office. Wettermark was confident that Lewis would show his future constituents no more consideration or respect than he had the troops under his command. The people's loss would be the army's gain. A career military man, Wettermark could scarcely wait for Lewis to move on to bigger things.

"It doesn't make any sense, sir," said Wettermark. "Why would one man come in here and take on a whole regiment? And who shot this woman? Was she armed?"

"She got caught in the crossfire. And I don't know what

that bastard she was with intended by coming here, but he killed four of my men and I want his scalp. It doesn't look good, Captain. First the ambush, and now this."

"It may be," said Wettermark, "that this man, this Confederate, wasn't riding with the guerrillas at all."

"What do you mean by that?"

"Maybe he was just passing through, Colonel. The war is over in the east. We can expect some Confederates to pass through this region on their way west."

"If they make the mistake of passing through here I'll hang them," growled Lewis.

Wettermark shook his head.

"Do you have a problem with that, Captain?" snapped Lewis.

"Yes, sir. I do. Was this man wearing a uniform?"

"No, he was not. What does that prove? Most of the partisans don't. But this man *had* a uniform with him. It was rolled up in a blanket. Along with this."

Lewis walked around to the other side of the coffin. A sword and scabbard lay across the sawhorses beside the coffin—Wettermark couldn't see it from where he was standing. Lewis picked it up and tossed it to him. Wettermark examined it closely.

"This is the sword of an officer in the regular army," he said. "I haven't seen many partisan rangers carry a sword like this."

"Look here, Wettermark," said Lewis, exasperated. "You need concern yourself with only one thing. I want you to track this man down."

"Why me, Colonel?"

"Because you were born out here in this Godforsaken frontier. You can track better than an Indian. And, finally, because I damn well said so."

"Excuse me, gents." The blacksmith put the lid on the coffin and began to nail it down. Wettermark wondered where the young woman had come from, and if she had any family. If so, they would never know that she had ended up in a dusty nameless grave on the Missouri prairie.

"You will leave in the morning. By the way, the man was wounded. I don't know how badly. Any questions?"

"One, sir. I'd like to take this sword along."

"Fine. Use it on the bastard. Only don't come back without him. Do I make myself clear, Captain?"

"Perfectly clear, sir."

With a curt nod Colonel Lewis left the livery. Wettermark lingered. He figured someone ought to be there when the young woman was laid to rest. Maybe he would say a few words—if he could remember the right ones.

That night, many miles from Franklin, Dalton finally stopped. Neither he nor the coyote dun could go any further. He found some cover in shrub willows clinging to life on the rocky banks of a trickling stream. Both he and the horse had a badly needed drink. Before he passed out, Dalton had the presence of mind to tie the reins securely around his arm.

The sun in his face woke him the following morning. He felt terrible. The bullet had to come out, and soon. He had no way to do it himself,, so he had to find a doctor. There was grave risk involved in that course of action. The Yankees knew he had been wounded in the Franklin scrape—they would surmise that he would seek the help of a physician. But he had no choice. If the bullet was not removed, he would die.

His problem was that he was unfamiliar with this country, and had no idea in which direction the nearest town lay. So he headed due north, and about noon came upon a well-traveled wagon road, angling east-west across the prairie sea of grass. He turned west, and by mid-afternoon found himself on the main street of a small, dusty town. It was as far as he could go. Slipping from the saddle, he passed out.

Regaining consciousness a few minutes later, he found himself being carried by three men. They transported him into a doctor's office. The doctor told the men to leave. As soon as the trio was gone, Dalton pulled the Schofield from his belt and aimed it at the sawbones. The latter looked down the barrel of the big revolver with remarkable aplomb.

"Funny way to ask for help."

"I'm not asking. Get the bullet out."

"I won't operate with a gun to my head."

"Then give me a knife and I'll do it."

"No. I perform the surgery in this office. Just put the gun away. You don't need it. You are safe here."

"It's not safe for me anywhere."

"Here you are safe," insisted the doctor. "I don't care who you are or what you have done. It is my duty to try to save your life."

"Tell that to the soldiers when they come. Maybe they'll listen—before they arrest you."

"I am not concerned with my own welfare at the moment, but yours. Now, will you put the gun down?"

Dalton lowered the Schofield. It was getting too heavy to hold up anyway. He had to trust this man.

When the thin steel probe entered the bullet hole and struck the slug, Dalton mercifully passed out again.

He came to in a comfortable bed, his midsection tightly encased in a clean white dressing. An elderly woman was sitting in a chair in the corner, reading her Bible. Seeing Dalton's eyes open, she smiled, rose, and left the room. A moment later the doctor entered.

"How long have I been unconscious?" asked Dalton. There was one window in the room, and all he could tell was that it was either dawn or dusk.

"Just a few hours."

"I've got to get moving."

"Don't be a fool. You need to stay in bed at least a week. You lost a great deal of blood. How far did you travel with that bullet in you?"

"I don't know. About a day."

The doctor shook his head. "You must have a very strong will and a high tolerance for pain."

"Is the bullet out?"

"Oh yes. I couldn't help but notice your scars. This wasn't the first time you have been shot. You were in the war, I take it."

"I still am."

"I see."

"Where are my clothes?"

"On the trunk at the end of your bed. Your gun, too."

Dalton sat up. The pain made his head spin.

"I urge you in the strongest possible terms not to exert yourself. You will start bleeding again."

"I've got to go. They can't be far behind."

"Then, if you insist, I will help you."

Once he was dressed, Dalton produced some greenbacks—the last of the money Mrs. Crenshaw had paid him back in West Virginia. "How much do I owe you?"

"Let me ask you something. Why are you still fighting? Don't you know that the war is over?"

"Yes, I know," rasped Dalton. "I was willing to let it be over, too. But the Yankees weren't. They killed my . . . my wife. So I killed as many of them as I could. And with any luck I'll kill a lot more before they get me."

"You should just let it be. Revenge is a double-edged sword."

"I can't let it be." The image of Margaret, lying dead in a pool of her own blood, tormented Dalton. His eyes blazed with naked malice. "I'll never let it be."

"Where will you go?"

"West. Into the mountains. And when I'm healed, I'll come back down out of those mountains and finish what I started."

"You intend to take on the entire United States Army all by yourself?"

"Are you enlisting, Doc?"

The sawbones smiled. "No. Keep your money. I'll go get your horse." At the door he turned back. "God have mercy on your soul, my friend."

The next morning, early, Captain Wettermark knocked on the door to the doctor's office.

"I understand you treated a Rebel officer," he said.

The doctor glanced beyond Wettermark at the column of bluecoat cavalry in the street. They were scanning the town with their carbines ready. Fortunately, thought the doctor, there wasn't a soul in sight. He was afraid the troopers might shoot the first thing that moved.

"He is gone. He left last night. So, if you don't mind, Captain, tell your men to relax."

Wettermark was peering over the doctor's shoulder, into the office.

"If you don't believe me," said the physician, "you are welcome to search the premises."

Wettermark gave him a long, searching look. "That won't be necessary. Did he tell you anything?"

"He said your men killed his wife. That the war was over for him until that happened. I can see in your face, Captain, that he told the truth."

Wettermark sighed. "I'm afraid so."

"I can also see that your men are trigger-happy."

"That's to be expected, don't you think, when at any moment a shopkeeper could turn into a partisan and take a shot at them? Did he tell you where he was going?"

"West, into the mountains. He told me because he

wants you to follow him. But I don't think you're going to catch this man, Captain, until he wants you to."

"I'll catch him. I have to. Those are my orders. Thanks, doctor."

Wettermark stepped off the boardwalk and went to his horse.

"No matter how long it takes?" asked the doctor.

Swinging lithely into the saddle, Wettermark said, "No matter if it takes ten hours or ten years, I'll catch up with him. You see, I have something that belongs to him, and I want to be the one to return it, personally."

11

Crossing the Clearwater River, Dalton urged his coyote dun up a steep slope, through a stand of longleaf pine and then to the top of a bluff covered with sun-yellowed grass tall enough to brush the horse's belly. At the crest he halted the dun and scanned his backtrail with a bleak gaze.

Way off to the east he saw a herd of elk grazing, but that and a hawk soaring high overhead were the only living things he could see. No sign for over a fortnight of the Yankees who had pursued him all the way from Missouri. Hadn't been for a while now. They might have finally given up the chase back on the arid sagebrush plains of eastern Colorado. That was where he had last seen them. There he had turned north, crossing the silvered shallows of the South Platte, thence to the North Platte, which he had followed west into more barren wasteland, the Great Basin. Reaching the Green River, he headed north again, into the very heart of the Rocky Mountains, and now, finally, he was on the high plains west of the Bitterroot Range.

It was beautiful country. Forested, snow-capped mountains, high prairies with undulating hills, a sea of sun-ripened grass rippling in the cool wind. Deep canyons and rocky escarpments, sparkling rivers and fertile valleys. The land was filled with game, the cold, fast-running streams inhabited by salmon and other fish in abundance. Dalton wanted to stay here for a spell. Not because he had an eye for the beauty of the land—a man on the run seldom had the chance to enjoy his surroundings—but rather because he was tired of running, tired to the very marrow of his bones. Now he was turning at bay.

The Yankees had demonstrated extraordinary tenacity in their pursuit of him. They had been hot on his trail for more than a month, across Missouri and Kansas and Colorado. On several occasions they had come very close to trapping him. In those days he had been slowed by the wound in his side. The wound was well on the way to being healed now, though it had been touch and go there for a while.

Many days had passed since the fight at Franklin. Margaret lay cold in her grave twelve hundred miles away. His heart seemed to twist itself into a painful knot every time she crossed his mind, which was at least once a minute. They said that time was the great healer. Dalton wondered how long it would take before he could think of Margaret without feeling like he was dying. His grief was still overpowering—and so was his rage. Often he had come perilously close to turning on his pursuers and having it out. But reason always prevailed. He knew he stood no chance against them. They would kill him for certain. He didn't want to give them the satisfaction. Not just yet. He was going to make them pay for what they had done—and to make them pay he had to pick and choose the time and place for the reckoning.

But now, after six weeks of running, he was tired. It was late summer. Before long the first snows would fall. He needed to find a place to hole up, a place where he could sit out the winter. He wanted to rest and recuperate and plan the first campaign of his one-man war against the United States Army, to be launched in the spring. In the fiery crucible of his consuming hate he would forge a steel resolve which would see him through to the bitter end. He would choose the time and the place for that, too, when he had decided that the United States had suffered and bled enough for robbing him of his future. Margaret Talcott had given him a purpose, a reason to live, after the bitter defeat of the Confederacy—now that she was gone, vengeance had become his reason for living. It was all he had left. He couldn't let go.

For half an hour he sat the coyote dun on the crest of the windswept hill, searching the undulating hills where the blue shadows of white clouds chased each other across the golden grass. The dun cropped greedily at the grass. Dalton knew he had been lucky chancing upon the dun back there in Franklin. The horse was a young, wiry mustang and could run like the wind—and it had been doing an awful lot of running the past two months.

Dalton concluded that the men who had tracked him from Franklin were no longer giving chase. But that didn't mean he could let down his guard, or stop glancing over his shoulder every other minute. Far as he knew, there wasn't a town for a hundred miles in any direction. That, however, did not mean there weren't any bluecoat soldiers in the vicinity. This was Indian country, which meant there were more army posts than towns anyway.

The Indians were another concern. Many tribes had seized the opportunity offered by the war the whites were waging among themselves to strike back at the American interlopers. The Comanche, Cheyenne, Pawnee, Paiute, Arapaho, and Sioux tribes had taken to the warpath, and the frontier was aflame. Dalton had no idea what tribes roamed this particular neck of the woods, but he had to assume that they were hostile, and they would probably make no distinction between the blue uniforms of the United States cavalry and his blood-stained tunic of butternut-gray.

With this in mind he proceeded with all due caution. That was the first and last time he silhouetted himself on the rim of high ground. He kept to the draws and the valleys, and avoided open ground as much as possible.

It was mid-afternoon when he heard the gunfire, coming from up ahead, beyond the next rise. He checked the dun sharply and listened with an experienced ear. Four or five rifles. Curiosity got the better of him. He kicked his horse into motion and rode up a steep, grassy incline, stopping shy of the crest. Dismounting, he ground-hitched the dun. The horse was well trained, and he was confident it would not stray. At a crouch he moved to the rim, and went the last few feet on hands and knees through the tall grass.

In the draw below he saw a single Indian, lying behind a dead horse, shooting up into the trees which covered the opposite slope. Dalton could not at first spot the Indian's adversaries, but he saw muzzle flash in the shade of the trees, and a wisp of powdersmoke. Could they be bluecoats? Dalton checked the rimrock above the trees. That was when he saw the Indian holding four—no, make that five—horses.

He was disappointed. No U.S. cavalry here. This lead-slinging quarrel was between Indians. He had no idea why they were shooting at each other and he didn't care. It was none of his concern. He left the rim and returned to the coyote dun. As expected, the horse was right where he had left it, cropping at the lush grass. Both the dun and Dalton had learned that when you were on the run you ate and drank whenever the opportunity presented itself. Usually,

the opportunities were few and far between. Dalton realized he was famished. He had a couple of hours of daylight
left—and he needed to find a good, secluded campsite and
something to eat.

Swinging into the saddle, he was about to turn the coyote dun back down the hill when the shooting intruded
on his thoughts and pricked his conscience. Five to one—
those were the odds against the lone Indian, pinned down
out in the open at the bottom of that draw. Those odds
offended his sense of fair play, which was strongly developed, largely as consequence of the fact that he and his
fellow Confederates had usually been sorely outnumbered themselves.

Dalton cursed under his breath. What he was contem-
plating—buying in on the side of the lone Indian—was
downright foolhardy. For one thing he knew nothing
about the situation. It was quite possible that the lone
Indian deserved to be in his present predicament. For
another, there was every likelihood that even if he managed to save that Indian's neck a bullet might be all the
thanks he got. Dalton sat there for a couple of minutes
trying to talk himself out of interfering. But it was no use.

Keeping to the low ground, he rode around behind the
hill to the west—to the rear of the Indian horse holder up
in the rimrock. He left the dun in a thicket and started to
climb. The fact that he had no rifle dictated this strategy.
With a long gun he might have been able to drive them
off from a distance. But all he had was a Schofield, so he
had to get in close.

He reached the granite brow of the hill and crept
through the weathered rocks, positioning himself above
and behind the horse holder. The Indian didn't have a
clue he was there—his attention was glued to the fight
going on down the hill. Dalton had a clear shot, and lined
up the Schofield. Then he realized how young the Indian

was. Just a boy—which perhaps explained why he had been chosen to hold the ponies while the others went off to get the glory.

Dalton had seen boys not much older than this Indian lad fight and die on the battlegrounds back east. But he could not bring himself to shoot this boy down. So he descended from the rocks, hoping to get in close enough to knock him out.

It didn't work. The ponies sensed Dalton and whickered a warning to the Indian. The boy's eyes got big when he saw Dalton. But he didn't run. Instead, dropping the bridle ropes and whipping a bone-handled knife from his belt, he launched himself at Dalton with a shrill war cry.

Startled, Dalton fired. He did not have time to even think about stopping the boy with a bullet in the leg. In that split second he shot to kill, because it was that or be killed. The bullet hit the Indian youth squarely in the chest and slammed him to the ground. The ponies scattered, some into the rocks, some down the slope into the trees.

"Damn it," muttered Dalton, staring bleakly at the boy.

He did not dwell long on the killing. There were four more Indians to deal with, and he was fairly sure they would know, now that he had fired a shot, that they had an enemy above them. The knife had been the boy's only weapon. Bad luck—Dalton had hoped to confiscate a rifle.

Starting down into the trees, he spotted one of the Indians working his way up the slope. Dalton fired, but the Indian was too quick for him, ducking out of sight behind the trunk of a longleaf pine, then answering with a shot that whistled so close to Dalton he thought he felt the breeze of the bullet's passing. At that moment he lost his footing and he toppled forward. The Indian thought he had hit his mark and charged forward. Dalton rolled over on his back, aimed, and fired.

The dead Indian's rifle proved to be a single shot percussion Hawken, a buffalo gun, a powerful weapon. Dalton searched the dead man's beaded and fringed buckskin shot pouch and powderhorn. Finding cartridge, cap, and plenty of gunpowder, he reloaded the big .50 caliber rifle and searched the woods for another target. The sun was going down, and the shadows were deepening. For the moment all the shooting had ceased. A tense silence reigned. Dalton didn't dare move or make a sound. His eyes straining to pierce the sudden gloom, he listened hard for a telltale noise.

The crack of a twig was as loud as a cannon's report to his ears. He spun, crouching, caught a brief glimpse of an Indian lunging at him—startlingly close. Then the Indian disappeared in a cloud of white powdersmoke as the Hawken jumped violently in his hands. As the smoke dissipated, Dalton saw the Indian sprawled on the ground, a big, bloody hole in his chest.

A bullet plucked the sleeve of his gray tunic. A blood-curdling shriek shattered the gray twilight. Dalton turned, and as he did so he threw down the empty Hawken and tugged the Schofield out of his belt. The Indian was charging straight at him, raising his own empty rifle like a club. Dalton knew he was not going to get the shot off in time. It was uncanny, how these warriors could get so close without him knowing.

Another rifle spoke. The charging Indian plunged face down at Dalton's feet and lay still.

Thirty yards downslope stood the Indian who had previously been pinned down in the draw. He quickly reloaded his rifle before coming forward. This gave Dalton time to get a good look at him. He was a tall, slender man, younger than Dalton. His black hair hung long to his shoulders, square cut, with an hourglass-shaped forelock which reached the bridge of his nose. His sun-bronzed features were angular. The buckskins he wore were plain, unadorned but for a bone breastplate.

Dalton kept the Schofield ready, not knowing what to expect. But as the Indian came closer Dalton saw that the rifle was shoulder-racked, and the man wore an amiable smile.

"I am called Toohoolzote," said the Indian, and his English was better than Dalton's. "I owe you my life. These Shoshone dogs ambushed me. They were closing in for the kill when you intervened." Toohoolzote's smile widened at the look of pure astonishment on Dalton's face. "You are perhaps wondering how it is that I speak your tongue so well. I have the Reverend to thank for that."

"The Reverend?"

"Yes. The Reverend Williams. He teaches us English at the mission station."

"What kind of Indian are you?"

"Nez Percé. And you are a graycoat, a long way from home."

"I have no home," said Dalton curtly, and changed the subject. "I took care of three of them. This one is yours. But I think that leaves one unaccounted for."

"No, I accounted for him."

Dalton nodded. He glanced grimly back up the hill. "One of them was just a boy."

Toohoolzote could see that Dalton carried a burden of remorse. "Did he die bravely?"

"He was very brave."

"Then do not feel bad, Graycoat. He will be greatly honored by his ancestors when he reaches the Other World. It is the prayer of every warrior that he die bravely in battle."

Dalton turned away. "I'll be going, then."

"Wait," said Toohoolzote. "You have traveled a long

and difficult road. I have some jerky and camas bread. I will share this with you."

Dalton wasn't sure how far he could trust Toohoolzote. It occurred to him that the Indian might want to share a night camp with him for the purpose of making off with his horse. But in the end Dalton decided to risk it. He was hungry. Besides, after six weeks on the run, it would be good to have someone to talk to. The coyote dun was a good listener, but . . .

12

They built a small fire down in a hollow among the pines. The night was cold, and Dalton was glad for the warmth the fire provided. True to his word, Toohoolzote shared his food, strips of sun-cured elk meat and powder from the camas lily bulb which, when mixed with a little water, made a rather tasteless but filling paste. A meal had never tasted so good to Dalton, who had spent the last six weeks eating catch-as-catch-can—an occasional rabbit or sage hen, even snake on one occasion, whatever he could bag with the Schofield.

He had a Hawken rifle now, and he thought it would come in real handy as he set about hunting a supply of meat to last him the winter. Being from the deep South, he did not know a lot about winter survival techniques, but he figured he had better learn damned quick up here in the high country. If the summer nights were this cool, he shuddered to think what winter would bring.

Toohoolzote explained that he had been returning to his village from a visit with the Cayuses, cousins of the Nez Percé who lived to the west. The Nez Percé, the Cayuse, and the Palouse all spoke the same tongue, and were related by a long and fruitful history of intertribal marriage. The Shoshones, along with the Bannocks and the Paiutes, sometimes sent raiding parties north to steal Nez Percé horses—and sometimes Nez Percé girls. They were the *Tewelka*, the "enemy to be fought." It had been so for many generations. Toohoolzote had been unlucky in crossing paths with one such party. They had shot his "Sunday" horse. He was shocked by Dalton's suggestion that they cut some steaks from the dead pony.

"I could no more eat that horse than I could another human being," said Toohoolzote, and then flashed that winning smile. "You white men truly are barbarians."

Dalton had to laugh at that. "Funny. And we think of you as savages."

Despite his initial wariness, Dalton quickly took a liking to the loquacious, good-natured Nez Percé. Toohoolzote told him that his band had its summer camp a half day's ride to the northeast, at Musselshell Meadow. Here, while the women dug for a year's supply of camas lily bulbs, the men joined the Flatheads and the Kutenais and the Crows in buffalo hunts, ranging far across the northern plains.

"Then why aren't you out hunting buffalo?" asked Dalton.

"I am not a very good hunter, I'm afraid. Or fighter, for that matter. I am a storyteller. A song singer. My mother was a *tewat*, a shamaness. When I was nine I was taken to the top of a mountain and left there, alone, to seek a vision. My guardian spirit, my *wey-ya-kin*, was the Coyote. Our people know many legends about the Coyote, who has great powers. If the Coyote likes you, you will want for nothing. But if you have done something to annoy him, he can bring great misfortune down upon you. Because the Coyote is my *wey-ya-kin*, people come to me and ask me to sing songs for them. You see, singing pleases the Coyote, and a good song for someone will make the Coyote more inclined to give that person the favor he seeks."

"If that's true," mused Dalton, "then I guess I've annoyed the Coyote plenty."

"I would be happy to sing a song for you. It is the least I can do for the man who saved my life. What is it that you wish?"

"A cabin. A place to spend the winter, where I will be left alone."

"And where the yellowlegs cannot find you?"

"Yellowlegs?"

"The soldiers. They wear a yellow stripe down the pegs of their trousers."

"What makes you think I'm hiding from the soldiers?"

"You wear the graycoat, still, even though the war is over. And you are still on the warrior's path. One need only look at you to see that this is so."

Dalton nodded. "I am still at war. They killed my wife. Well, we weren't exactly married, but we were going to be. They shot her down, for no reason, and now I will fight them until the day I die."

"I am truly sorry," said Toohoolzote. "As for the cabin, I do not need to sing a song for that. I know of just such a place."

"You do?"

"Yes. It is not far—about a day's ride from here, west towards the Snake River. I think a trapper once lived there. But that must have been long ago. You will not be bothered there."

"Sounds like just what I'm looking for."

"I will take you there. But first we must go to my village. My people will want to thank you for saving my life."

"I don't want any thanks."

"Still, we must go, before I take you to the cabin. It is on Nez Percé land, and you must have permission to live there. I am sure that permission will be granted. It is just a formality. All the people must see you, Graycoat, so that they will know you are a friend and must be left alone."

Dalton agreed.

He spent four days in the Nez Percé village on the Musselshell Meadow. Toohoolzote rarely left his side, acting as interpreter and guide. Thanks to the song singer, Dalton learned a lot about the tribe during his brief stay.

According to Toohoolzote, in the beginning there were no *la-te-tel-wit*—humans—in the world, only animals endowed with human qualities. One of these was the Coyote. When the Coyote learned that a Monster that lived near the Clearwater River was killing all the other animals and eating them, he ventured bravely forth to make things right. Tricking the Monster into swallowing him, the Coyote started a fire in the Monster's belly. When the Monster was dead, the Coyote carved its body into pieces and scattered these throughout the land. The pieces became the different Indian tribes. Finally the Coyote sprinkled the land where the Monster had lived with its blood, and from the Monster's blood sprang the *Ne-Mee-Po*—"The People"—now known as the Nez Percé.

Dalton was surprised to learn that there was no main chief in the village. The people selected a council, which in turn picked a headman, who was guided by the council's advice. The headman was sometimes a shaman also, but always he had to be wise, generous, brave, and diplomatic. His job was to settle disputes and lead by example. He could not overrule a decision of the council. The council was the real power in the village. It planned the hunting and gathering expeditions, and decided issues concerning the band's relationship with other tribes or bands. Both the headman and the council had limited authority. Neither could force an individual to do something he did not want to do. They ruled by persuasion. Since they were chosen by the people, and always had the welfare of the people foremost in their mind, the people usually went along with their decisions.

It was up to the council whether Dalton could live on Nez Percé land. As Dalton's advocate, Toohoolzote was very persuasive. There were a few members of the council who were concerned lest Dalton's war become their own. The Nez Percé were at peace with the *Shoyapee*, the white men. It had always been so. While other tribes had taken to the warpath and fought the yellowleg soldiers, the Nez Percé never had. But none could deny that the whole tribe owed Dalton a great debt for saving the life of the song singer. It took two full days of deliberation for the council to make up its mind. Dalton learned that an Indian was never in a hurry when it came to making an important decision. The verdict: Dalton could stay, for the time being.

Each Nez Percé village was independent, but those in a particular region were united into a band. So, in the tribe, there were the Wallowa Nez Percé, and the White Bird, the Salmon River, and the Asotin. Representatives from different villages made up the band council. The band unified the villages for mutual defense. The different bands were then unified in a confederacy, governed by a council made up of the headmen of each band. There was no head chief or permanent council at this level, but there did exist a war chief. This individual, elected by the headmen, became the supreme authority in times of war.

The Nez Percé lived in longhouses covered with mats fashioned of reeds and grass in their permanent camps. Some of these structures were a hundred feet long, and each accommodated at least two, and often more, families. But the camp at Musselshell Meadow was a temporary one, and here skin lodges had been erected.

The men customarily wore moccasins, leggings, breech-clouts, and sometimes a buckskin tunic, while the women were clad in belted dresses with long shirts and knee-length moccasins. The garb was ordinarily undecorated. On special occasions, men and women wore garments decorated with beads, bone, shell, dyed porcupine quills, elk's or bear's teeth, and the fur of ermine and wolf. Almost all adults regularly painted their faces. This, Toohoolzote explained to Dalton, was not only for protection against the sun or the cold or insects, but also to appeal to the opposite sex. Dalton noticed too that both men and women had their ears pierced, and wore strings of shells and bones or beads as earbobs. A few of the elders had pierced the septum of their nose and wore a decorative shell or bone there. This practice, which was dying out, was why the French Canadian trappers had taken to calling the *Ne-Mee-Po* the Nez Percé, or Pierced Nose.

The Nez Percé were hunters and fishermen. They practiced very little agriculture, although the white missionaries were trying to convert them to farming. They harvested sockeye, silver, dog, blueback, and chinook salmon from the rivers, as well as steelhead, sturgeon, and eel. They used spears, nets, hooks, and weirs made of brush and poles for this purpose. In the spring and summer, when the bands moved down to the plateaus, the women used digging tools to take large quantities of ripened roots from the ground, chief among them the camas, but also one called *toe-lup-kuht*, which hunters always took with them because it gave them strength and kept them mentally alert. The women also collected berries, and Dalton was astonished by the variety—blackberries, huckleberries, thornberries, serviceberries, and chokeberries. Pine nuts and sunflower seeds were also plentiful. Nuts and berries were made into cakes or used to flavor fish and meat.

Hunting parties went forth seeking bison, deer, elk, antelope, and bear, as well as grouse, geese, and sage hens. Dalton noticed that there were few firearms in the village. The Nez Percé hunter relied chiefly on his bow and arrows. The former was fashioned from syringa, thornbush, or cherrywood, strengthened with sinew. A few of the more fortunate carried a highly prized bow made from the horns of the mountain sheep, straightened by being boiled and then backed with sinew. Arrows were sometimes tipped in rattlesnake venom. Dalton was impressed by the power and durability of these weapons. When given the chance to try his hand with them, he proved to be a natural, which pleased and impressed his hosts no end.

A hunter did not hunt for his family alone, but rather for the village as a whole. All food was shared. Selfishness was an unacceptable vice among the Nez Percé. Parents used myths—many of which focused on creatures that were turned to stone if they did wrong—to teach their children Nez Percé customs and values. Bravery, generosity, self-discipline, and self-reliance were emphasized. Four short days were all that was needed to endow Dalton with a healthy respect and abiding admiration for the *Ne-Mee-Po*.

On Dalton's last day in the village, Reverend Williams arrived. The missionary was a scowling, ascetic man clad in a long, black frock coat and flat-brimmed Quaker's hat. Dalton took an immediate dislike to him. Williams struck him as an imperious and intolerant man, quick to find fault with everyone else. He doled out fire and brimstone at the drop of a hat, and chastised the Indians for their pagan ways at every opportunity, excoriating the handful he had managed to convert to an indifferent sort of Christianity for being absent so long from the mission.

Dalton got the distinct impression that many of the Nez Percé disapproved of Williams. The elders resented the fact that the missionary was trying to turn the people away from their traditional beliefs. But of course, the Nez Percé were nothing if not the perfect hosts, and never betrayed their hostility.

Toohoolzote genuinely liked Williams. The song singer thought the reverend was very brave, considering the fate which had befallen his predecessors.

Thirty years ago, two missionaries had been dispatched by the American Board of Commissioners for Foreign Missions for the purpose of learning how open the Indians in the area might be to proselytizing. They were Samuel Parker and Marcus Whitman. The Nez Percé were hospitable, and seemed to enjoy the religious services the two men conducted. Whitman went so far as to take two Nez Percé boys back east with him, in order to instruct them in English. Two headmen, Tackensuatis and Aleiya, the latter of whom became known as The Lawyer, were among the most enthusiastic disciples of the missionaries. Both had been wounded at the battle of the Teton Basin in 1832, when the Nez Percé had joined the mountain men holding a rendezvous at Pierre's Hole to repel a Blackfoot attack.

The two men returned the following year with their families. Whitman established his mission among the Cayuse Indians, on the Walla Walla River. Parker and a young couple, Henry and Eliza Spalding, settled among the Nez Percé near the mouth of Lapwei Creek.

The Nez Percé became attached to Eliza Spalding, a kind and gentle woman. Mr. Spalding managed to persuade some of the Indians to try their luck with gardens and orchards. But he was a stern and impatient man, who had a knack for antagonizing the shamans, whom he condemned as wicked sorcerers, and he displayed intolerance for most Indian customs. Perceiving himself as the savior of the Nez Percé, he exploded into violent anger when the Indians did not do what he wanted. More and more of the Nez Percé turned away from the missionaries as a result of Spalding's antics.

Meanwhile, the Whitmans had fared no better among the Cayuse, offending many of the Indians by insisting that they adopt the laws and ways of the white man, and selecting a head chief, whom the missionaries sought to manipulate, and by so doing control the entire tribe. Henry Spalding tried the same thing. The Nez Percé and their Cayuse cousins tried to comply, but the seeds of discord were soon planted, and swiftly developed into a rift between those who resented the activities of the missionaries and those who were trying to become Christians.

It became increasingly clear that the white man did not abide by the very laws he sought to impose on the Indians—a headman was murdered by an unscrupulous trader, and the murderer got off scot free. Perhaps worse, more and more immigrants were streaming into Cayuse and Nez Percé land. One such group, bound for the Willamette Valley, spread measles among the Cayuses. The epidemic killed half the tribe. A rumor spread that the missionaries were intentionally poisoning their Indian flock so that their white brethren could take the land.

In November 1847, the Indians struck. Cayuses killed Marcus Whitman and eleven other whites at the mission. At Lapwei, the Spaldings and a few others were taken hostage by the Nez Percé, who feared American soldiers would march against them in reprisal for the killings. Eventually the hostages were ransomed by Peter Skene Ogden, a Hudson Bay Company man, a trusted friend of the Indians, and were escorted out of the region by fifty Nez Percé.

Both missions were looted and burned to the ground. The whites did launch a punitive expedition. Volunteers from the settlements in the Willamette Valley marched on the Indians. The Cayuses asked the Nez Percé to join them in defending their homeland. The Nez Percé believed that the only way to protect their land and themselves was to remain on peaceful terms with the Americans. As it happened, the Cayuses did not need the Nez Percé. The white volunteers mistakenly attacked the Palouses, who whipped them soundly and sent them packing back to the Willamette.

Ten years later Reverend Williams arrived. Some of Spalding's converts, like The Lawyer, had continued to live as Christians, and welcomed Williams. The others, though they had not forgotten the problems which the Whitmans and the Spaldings had made for them, nonetheless were firm in their conviction that the wisest course was to remain on good terms with the *Shoyapee*.

"Are you a Christian?" Dalton asked Toohoolzote.

"I have read the Bible, and sometimes I attend services, but I have not been converted to the Christian faith."

"In the Gospels," said Dalton, "it says to turn the other cheek. Let me tell you something. If you and your people keep turning the other cheek to the United States, you'll lose your lands."

Toohoolzote shook his head. "We have a treaty. It says the Nez Percé will live here on their land forever."

He explained to Dalton about the Council of 1855. Isaac Stevens, the Superintendent for Indian Affairs and a politically ambitious man who wanted to be known as the man who made the transcontinental railroad a reality, had wanted to bring peace to the plains and end the Indian threat to expansion. He persuaded the headmen of all the bands of all the tribes east of the Cascades to meet in the Walla Walla Valley in the spring of 1855. The Nez

Percé nation, the Cayuses, the Palouses, the Umatillas, Yakimas, and other tribes sent representatives to the council and listened to what Stevens had to say.

Stevens was counting on the friendly Nez Percé to swing the other, more distrustful tribes over to the cause of peace. The arrival of the Nez Percé contingent was encouraging. Led by Aleiya, The Lawyer, who carried the Stars and Stripes, the Nez Percé entered the encampment at a gallop and entertained those already present with a series of dazzling equestrian displays.

Starting out on the wrong foot, Stevens told the Indians that the United States government had made tribes like the Cherokees happy and prosperous by moving them to new, rich lands west of the Mississippi River.

"We knew that was untrue," said Toohoolzote. "Half-bloods had come through our land and spoken of the plight of the Cherokees and all the tribes in the east. Still, we wanted to have peace with the *Shoyapee*, so we let Stevens tell his lies."

"You should have gotten on your horses and rode away," said Dalton.

Stevens went on to tell the Indians about all the gifts the Americans would give them: blankets, kettles, brightly colored cloth, wagons, plows, and other farm implements, even sawmills, schools, and blacksmith shops. Finally he revealed his plan to create three reservations. One would be for the Yakimas and other tribes along the Columbia River. A second would be set aside for the Cayuses, the Wallawallas, Umatillas, and Spokans, while the third would be for the Nez Percé. The Nez Percé reservation included all of their ancestral lands. They gave up nothing, and so readily agreed to the arrangement. Other tribes, particularly the Cayuses and Wallawallas, had to give up their homelands.

"There were rumors," said Toohoolzote, "of a plot

among the Wallawallas to murder Stevens. But no harm came to him. The Nez Percé guarded him night and day until the council was over."

Dalton shook his head. "What about your cousins, the Cayuses. Didn't you care that they were getting the short end of the stick?"

Toohoolzote looked away. "They should not have killed the whites at the Whitman mission. The American hearts were hard against them because of that."

Dalton was distressed by the apparent pacifism of the Nez Percé. "That is not the way to deal with the United States, Toohoolzote. You've got to fight to keep what's yours."

"But we have kept what is ours without fighting. Graycoat, your own people were defeated by the United States. What chance would we have? We number only five thousand. How many yellowleg soldiers are there?"

"Hundreds of thousands."

"So you see, Graycoat, the reason we strive for peace."

Dalton sighed. "It's no good. Someday the United States will want your land. They will come and take it, and whether you are their friends or not won't make a damned bit of difference."

"I disagree. Other tribes have broken the treaties and gone on the warpath while the great war in the east raged. They will suffer because of it. But the Nez Percé have always kept their word. And so the Americans will keep theirs. There are no whites settling on Nez Percé land." The song singer smiled. "Except for one, now."

"Mark my words," said Dalton grimly. "You will rue the day you ever sat down and listened to their lies."

13

Dalton was in a hurry to leave the village. The Nez Percé were extremely hospitable, and he felt altogether welcome, yet seeing the happy families and the young couples courting only enlarged the hole in his heart made by the loss of Margaret. It had been very difficult for him, these past weeks, alone, on the run, but to his surprise he discovered that being in the presence of other people made it all that much harder to bear.

There was another reason. He wasn't sure the Reverend Williams could be trusted. He learned that the missionary was asking questions about him. Perhaps it was perfectly understandable, but perhaps there was more to it than mere curiosity. Toohoolzote told him not to worry. Williams would not make trouble for him. The reverend's only interest was saving Nez Percé souls. But Dalton wasn't convinced. And even if Williams didn't spread the word that a lone gray-coated rider was lingering among the Indians, there would be other whites, primarily traders, passing through sooner or later.

Early the next morning, Dalton and Toohoolzote departed on a three-day journey to the north and west. Their destination was a one-room cabin nestled in tall

pines at the back end of a box canyon near the confluence
of the Clearwater and Potlatch Rivers. Dalton took an
immediate liking to the spot. Toohoolzote informed him
that it was two day's ride from the nearest trading post or
mission, and more than a week from the closest army outpost. No well-traveled trail passed anywhere near. A creek
ran through the canyon, nourished by year-round springs
in the granite cliffs which loomed behind the cabin. There
was plenty of game. The cabin itself was in remarkably
good repair for a place that had been abandoned for years.
Dalton figured it would not take long to patch the holes in
the shingled roof and chink a few places in the walls. The
only furniture was a split-log table with a missing leg and
the frame of what had once been a rope-slat bed.
Toohoolzote had provided him with an axe, some rope,
some powder and shot for the Hawken rifle, and a sack of
food staples—camas flour, dried venison, salt, a little
sugar, and coffee bought from a trader.

The song singer stayed overnight. Sitting by the fire
built out in front of the cabin, he listened to the soughing
of the wind in the pines and shook his head.

"This is a lonely place," he decided. "Are you certain
you want to live here?"

"It suits me."

"I will come visit you now and then."

Dalton nodded. "Just make sure you watch out for
those Shoshones."

Toohoolzote laughed.

At sunrise the next day he took his leave. As they
shook hands, he said, "I think we have become good
friends in a short time, Graycoat."

"I agree. Take care of yourself, Toohoolzote. Sing a
song for me every now and then. I want the Coyote to like
me."

Dalton watched the Indian ride away, then turned to

gaze at the cabin. He figured this was as good a place as any to spend the winter. Here he would master the grief which gnawed away at his guts. Here he would plan a campaign against the Yankees for the following spring. Of course, he would leave Nez Percé country first. They wanted to live in peace with the United States, and he did not want to make trouble for them.

At that moment he had no idea that he would spend the next twelve years here.

His first order of business was to repair the cabin, and he made short work of that task. Then he set about laying in a supply of firewood for the long winter which lurked just around the corner. Wielding an axe brought back memories of his youth on that hardscrabble Alabama farm, the backbreaking labor from "can see" to "can't see," and all for what? By and large these were not fond memories, but the skills he had acquired in those days stood him in good stead now. He fastened a new leg onto the split-log table, strung the rope into the bed frame, and filled a buckskin mattress with sun-cured grass. He made a sturdy bench to go with the table, and a frame for stretching skins and drying meat.

Every day he saddled up the coyote dun and took a ride, intent on familiarizing himself with his environment, starting with the canyon first, acquainting himself with every nook and cranny, then venturing further afield, ranging as far as thirty miles in every direction. For two months he saw nary a living soul, and he liked it that way.

Toohoolzote visited him once more before the onslaught of winter, bringing him more salt, sugar, coffee, and a little tobacco. Dalton was glad to see the song singer, and pleased with the provisions. Now he would not have to be so stingy with the sugar and coffee already in his possession, and as for the tobacco, he resolved to make himself a pipe. The song singer also brought him a straight razor. Dalton wasted no time scraping the thick beard from his face—it had grown long and scraggly, and become a nest for varmints. But Toohoolzote's best gifts of all were a bow and some arrows and a Bible.

"When you visited our village you showed you can use this," said the Nez Percé as he gave Dalton the bow. "Now you can save your powder and shot, which is very difficult to come by."

This time Toohoolzote stayed several days. When it was time for him to go, the Nez Percé explained that his band was returning to the mountains, to their winter home, and that it would probably be spring before he could visit again.

"Is there anything you need?" he asked.

"No. Thanks to you I have everything I could want."

"You are certain?"

"Stop beating around the bush, Toohoolzote. What are you getting at?"

"Are you not lonely out here, Graycoat? Perhaps you could come live with us for the winter. You know you would be welcome."

Dalton shook his head. "Thanks for the offer, but no. I'll see you next year."

A month after Toohoolzote's visit the first snows came. It was bitterly cold, but Dalton was prepared. Having killed a buffalo a few weeks earlier, he had a nice warm buffalo skin and plenty of salted meat. Before long he was completely snowed in, but not before he had constructed a lean-to for the coyote dun, with room for the storage of bundles of dried grass. With plenty of food and firewood, and ice from the nearby creek, which had quickly frozen solid, for water, Dalton was comfortably well off. He whiled away the long days reading the Bible and trying his hand at fashioning a pair of snowshoes. The end result, in his opinion, wasn't half bad for an Alabama boy.

He had a lot of time to think as the snow fell to pile up high against the cabin walls, and the cold wind howled around the eaves. Eventually he cured himself of thinking about the "might-have-beens," had Margaret not been killed. He finally accepted the fact that she was gone. This was the first, essential step towards healing his emotional wounds. He started to sleep better, though she still sometimes haunted his dreams. In those dreams he relived every day they had spent together, from the moment he had first seen her on the veranda of the Talcott house, to the moment she fell, Yankee bullets in her, on the boardwalk in Franklin, Missouri—and then he would awaken, shattered, and have to knit himself back together again.

With the spring came Toohoolzote. This time he was not alone. A young Indian woman was with him. Dalton was glad to see the song singer, glad it was spring, glad the snow was melting and the creek running again and the game had come back. As usual, Toohoolzote had brought him salt, sugar, coffee, and tobacco.

"You are looking well, Graycoat," said the Nez Percé. "The winter was not too hard on you."

"Not at all. Is this your wife, Toohoolzote? She's very pretty."

Toohoolzote blushed, embarrassed. "No. Her name is Turns from the Light. She is an outcast, like you, my friend. I told her all about you and . . . well, we thought perhaps she could stay here with you for a while."

The smile froze on Dalton's face. "What do you mean, an outcast?"

"She was taken as child from the Bannocks. She has been with our band for fifteen summers. As you say, she is very pretty. Many young men have pursued her. But you must understand, it is—how do you say it?—not acceptable to marry a Bannock woman. Last winter, a man who has a wife and children made a fool of himself because of Turns from the Light. The council decided it was time for her to go. Personally, I disagree with their decision. She is not the one who should be punished. It was not her fault that she has the face of a flower and the slender form of a graceful willow. She never encouraged those men. She did nothing wrong or immoral. But the council has spoken. So be it."

"Why doesn't she just go back to the Bannocks?"

"The Bannocks have been our avowed enemies for many generations, Graycoat. They would never take her back, after she has been among the Nez Percé for so long. They would kill her, because she has been soiled by her long association with us. No, she cannot return to her people. She has no home. You know how that feels."

Dalton shook his head. "What are you trying to do, Toohoolzote? She can't stay with me."

"Why not?"

"Because I'm on the run. And at war, in case you've forgotten."

"I have not forgotten. But I had hoped you would forget."

"Well, I haven't," snapped Dalton. Immediately he felt bad for having spoken so curtly to his friend. "Listen, Toohoolzote. In a few weeks I will be leaving this place. I am going to try to kill Yankees, and they are going to be trying to kill me. I know you care about what happens to her. Surely you can see that would be no kind of life for a young woman."

"It is no kind of life for anyone. But I understand. I will take her away. Can I stay for a day or two?"

"Of course," said Dalton—and thereby doomed himself.

Toohoolzote stayed for nearly a week. During that

time he watched as Dalton slowly but surely changed his mind about Turns from the Light. Dalton fought it—fought it hard. At first he tried to ignore the Bannock girl. But Toohoolzote caught him sneaking glances at her. She was very slender and beautiful, with long glossy black hair, a heart-shaped face, limpid brown eyes, a shy and winsome smile. No man, mused the song singer, could long resist her charms. Even a man like Dalton. Toohoolzote could tell that his friend was not yet fully recovered from the loss of Margaret, but he had reconciled himself to the fact that she was dead, and was realizing that life marched inexorably on. And Turns from the Light was full of life, and the promise of life.

So it was that when Toohoolzote saw the time was right and expressed his intentions of leaving, Dalton told him the Bannock girl could stay. He made it sound as though he was reluctantly making a concession solely because she had nowhere else to go, as one would take in a stray dog out of compassion, but the song singer knew better. Dalton was smitten, in spite of himself. Maybe he did not love her. Yet. Perhaps that would come in time. Toohoolzote hoped so, because love was the best cure for hate.

As for Turns from the Light, she was happy with the arrangement. She had taken an immediate liking to Graycoat. Toohoolzote was quite pleased with himself as he rode away. He believed that the presence of Turns from the Light would eventually work to change Dalton's mind about his war of vengeance.

14

Dalton kept telling himself in the weeks that followed the arrival of Turns from the Light that he needed to launch his campaign against the Yankees. But each day he found some reason for delaying his departure. During the long winter he had depleted his supply of firewood and meat, and so he was obliged to go out with the axe and the bow and restock. Light—as he took to calling her— proved to be extremely handy when it came time for skinning the game and dressing it out. She made him a very fine buckskin hunting shirt. He was astonished. No one had ever done anything like that for him.

Although at first she spoke no English, he tried to teach her essential words, and was pleased to find her a quick study. Even so, she did not talk much. She was very quiet and unobtrusive as she went about her work with steady diligence. She was a hard worker. He ate much better now, because she collected the roots of the camas lily to make flour for bread, and berries which she made into jam, and honey from a bee tree down the canyon, and she even took fish out of the creek.

One warm spring day, returning from a hunt with an antelope across the coyote dun's saddle, Dalton came upon Light bathing in the creek. She did not know he was there. Dalton felt ashamed, but he could not help but stare. He had seen women, in the Richmond bordellos during the war, but they had not been attractive, as a rule. Light was a pure work of art. She had to be, he decided, the most beautiful living creature on the face of the earth, and even while the vision aroused him, there was more to it than that.

The rest of the day he was tormented by thoughts of Margaret, and he felt guilty for the feelings he now had for Light, and he did his utmost to exorcise those feelings, but could not. It was then that he resolved to leave, and told her that night—he would depart at daybreak. She accepted the news without comment, but he thought he caught a glimmer of dismay on her lovely face.

The following morning, as he was about to climb into the saddle and ride away she abruptly grabbed his arm.

"You come back?" She struggled with the unfamiliar words, and he knew she was pleading, not asking.

"Yes," he said gruffly, confused and angry at himself, because he did not really want to go after all, and by not wanting to he was betraying Margaret's memory. Pulling free of Light's grasp, he mounted up and rode away, forcing himself not to look back.

He rode for miles without paying the slightest attention to where he was going, struggling to sort through the turmoil in his heart and in his mind.

Margaret wouldn't want you to go through with this. . . .

He checked the coyote dun sharply as this revelation struck him. There wasn't the slightest doubt in his mind that this was so. She would not want him to waste his life on the vengeance trail. She would want him to live. To love. To be happy. She would want these things for him because she loved him.

Turning the horse around, he galloped back to the cabin. For some reason he was terribly afraid that Light might be gone. She had seemed convinced that he wasn't going to come back. . . .

But she was there. Came running out of the cabin to greet him. Dalton executed a running dismount and swept her up in his arms. She laughed—until he kissed her. That shocked her.

"What's the matter?" he asked. "Haven't you ever been kissed before? That was a kiss."

"Kiss," she echoed, and with her arms locked around his neck, pulled his face back down to hers.

Two months later, returning from a hunt on a hot summer day, Dalton saw a horse tied up in front of the cabin. The saddle rig was a McClellan, the blanket beneath it blue with a yellow stripe. Seeing this made Dalton's stomach tie itself up into a knot. That was standard issue for cavalry regiments of the United States Army.

Dalton's blood ran cold. His first thought was that somehow the Yankees had found him. Maybe Reverend Williams. But no. They would not have sent just one man. Maybe it was a trap. Dalton scanned the skyline. But that didn't make sense either. Why would they send in one man, to leave his horse in plain sight. Dalton decided in the end that it really didn't matter anyway. As far as he knew, Light was in the cabin, and he had to make sure she was okay. So he rode in. When he kicked the cabin door open he had his hand on the butt of the Schofield stuck in his belt.

A man in Yankee blue was standing over Light, who knelt before the fireplace, stirring the stew which bubbled in the iron kettle Toohoolzote had brought them on his most recent visit. The soldier was lanky, yellow-haired, unshaven. A corporal's stripes adorned his short tunic. He stepped away from Light, a leer frozen on his lips as he looked at Dalton. Light looked around, and Dalton could see the fear in her eyes, and thanked God Almighty he had not arrived any later.

"Who the hell are you?" he rasped, his blue eyes turning black with anger.

The man glanced at the Schofield, grinned crookedly, and held out his hands.

"No harm done, mister. Just passing through. Could smell this fine stew a mile downwind, and was mighty hungry, thought I'd stop in, see if I couldn't get a little something to eat."

"Get out."

"Now that ain't very hospitable. . . . "

"You're a deserter, aren't you?"

The lopsided grin vanished, and the man's pale eyes grew hard and cold. "What if I am?"

"It's none of my business. Just ride on."

"Yeah. I'm a deserter. Slipped out of Fort Lapwei a couple nights ago. To hell with the army. There's gold out here, and I aim to get me some. Hell, might even strike it rich. Find the mother lode. To hell with forty miles a day on beans and hay. Trying to keep folks off Indian land. I say kill all the red heathens and take the damned land. All except the purty ones, of course." He glanced across at Light, who had risen to move into the nearest corner, and the leer touched the corners of his mouth again.

"Look at her like that again and I'll have to kill you," said Dalton. His voice was deadly calm, matter-of-fact.

"She your squaw? Hell, Injun women are used to being passed around. I'll give you a dollar if you'll let me cover her."

Dalton itched to put a bullet right between the eyes of this yellowleg corporal. But he restrained himself, giving himself time to think through the consequences of the contemplated act.

"Not a chance," he said through clenched teeth.

"Well, I cain't hardly blame you for not wanting to share. She's the purtiest little red devil I think I've ever seen."

"There is no gold in these hills," said Dalton.

"There damn sure is. How would you know? You ain't no prospector. What are you doing out here, anyway?"

"Trying to mind my own business."

"You've got no business here," said the corporal, truculently. "This is Indian country. No white folks allowed." Then he chuckled. "Of course, that's not stopping too many of 'em. Ain't no concern of mine, anyhow. I'm just . . . "

Dalton pulled the Schofield and shot the man between the eyes.

The corporal's body slammed backwards, then bounced off the blood-splattered wall to pitch violently forward. Dalton glanced at Light. She gazed dispassionately at the corpse.

"I had to do it," said Dalton.

She nodded, knowing it was true, knowing—as Dalton had known—that sooner or later the corporal would have tried to kill Dalton just to have her.

Dalton took the man's pistol—a Schofield .45, just like his own—and ammunition pouch. Then he wrapped the corporal's tunic around the head to soak up some of the blood, and carried him a hundred yards up the canyon, where he buried him in a shallow grave.

When he got back to the cabin he found Light already at work scrubbing blood off the floor and wall.

"I'm going to take his horse and backtrack him a ways," said Dalton. "The army's probably out looking for him, and they might be using Indian trackers. I'll try to fix it so his sign doesn't lead anywhere near here."

She came to him and put her arms tightly around him, and he held her for a good long time, stroking her hair.

"Don't worry," said Dalton. "I promise I won't let anything happen to you."

A fortnight later Toohoolzote arrived for a visit. Dalton told him what had happened.

"I didn't kill him because he wore a blue uniform," said Dalton. "I just wanted you to know that."

"I am very glad that you have turned your back on vengeance, my friend."

"They won't find his body, so I don't think this will cause your people any trouble. After all, he was a deserter. If the Army had caught him he would have been executed anyway. But if you want me to leave, I will." Dalton glanced at Light. "We will."

"No. It could cause no more trouble than already exists."

Toohoolzote told them that gold *had* been discovered on Nez Percé land, up in the Walla Walla country, and thousands of prospectors were pouring in. The song singer feared that many thousands more were on their way. White settlements were springing up literally overnight. Merchants, confidence men, gamblers, and prostitutes were setting up shop in these "boom towns," trying to lure the miners into their canvas-walled dens and pick their pockets. The yellowlegs were completely ineffective in preventing this swarm of interlopers, who were infesting the traditional hunting and fishing grounds, like so many lice, scaring away the game and polluting the streams with their effluvium.

"This is just the beginning," warned Dalton. "Why don't your people do something?"

"A few have tried. But the headmen like Lawyer are stopping them."

"Stopping them? What for?"

"I am ashamed to say it. Some of the headmen prosper

because of the whites. One operates a ferry. Several others sell food and livestock to the *Shoyapee*. Lawyer has just signed an agreement which permits the prospectors to remain. In return, the government promises to pay the Nez Percé fifty thousand dollars. The land still belongs to the Nez Percé, and the whites are forbidden to go anywhere else on the reservation."

Dalton scoffed. "That agreement isn't worth spit, Toohoolzote. You should know that by now."

Toohoolzote nodded dismally. "Yes, I know it. For one thing, a piece of paper will not stop the whites from moving onto the rest of our land when they want to. For another, I doubt the headmen will ever see any of that fifty thousand dollars. We still have not received the money and other things the government promised at the Council of 1855. The Indian agents are corrupt. They steal the goods which are supposed to be given to us, and the money to be used for the mills and the schools we were expecting."

"I'm telling you," said Dalton. "You've got to fight."

"But we would lose that fight, Graycoat. They are too many. We are too few. What chance would we have? What good would it do?"

"The government is going to take your land. Are you going to just give it to them? Or will you fight them for it? Whether you win or lose is not the issue."

Toohoolzote sighed. "As long as headmen like Lawyer are alive there will be no war. But Lawyer is growing old. There is one man—his name is *Hin-mah-too-yah-lat-kekht*, Thunder Traveling to Loftier Mountain Heights. He is known by the Christian name of Joseph, as was his father before him. Joseph is now chief of the Wallowa Band. They were not at the Council of 1855. They have refused to sign any treaties, and do not recognize the right of headmen like Lawyer to speak for them. Do not misunderstand. Chief Joseph does not counsel taking the warpath. He is a peace-loving man, gentle and compassionate, eloquent in his call for peace, and slow to anger. But he insists that the whites should keep their word and get off our land, and many of the angry young men are flocking to him."

"What you need is a man who will lead your people into battle," persisted Dalton. "Make the government pay in blood for what they are going to steal from you anyway."

"You talk of making war against your own people, Graycoat."

"I have no people," said Dalton coldly, "and no country. All I have is this cabin, and Light, and your friendship, Toohoolzote."

"So you will stay."

"As long as I can."

"And if the time comes, will you fight with us, against the yellowlegs?"

"That's a fight I don't want to miss. I just hope you get around to it before I die of old age."

Toohoolzote smiled. "I hope it never happens. But then, I am not a warrior like you, Graycoat."

That evening Dalton stepped out of the cabin to smoke his pipe and gaze into the purple shadows which gathered in the low places between the golden hills. He wondered how long it would take for the Nez Percé to realize that if they wished to live their lives in their own way, and on their own land, then they would have to be willing to die for the right.

As for himself, he would live here with Light, in peace and solitude, and he would leave the world alone, until the world intruded on his happiness. This would happen, sooner or later. He was resolved to cherish every day until then.

Ten years passed. . . .

15

Major Ben Wettermark rode into Fort Lapwei on a hot summer's day in June 1877. His sorrel horse looked like it was on its last legs, but as usual Wettermark bore the appearance of a man who did not know the meaning of the word *fatigue*. His had been a very arduous trail. His uniform was gray with dust and grime. He was gaunt and sunburned and needed a bath and a shave, as he had been three weeks traveling across the high plains from Fort Laramie. But his eyes were still keen as he scanned the collection of log buildings built near a wooded creek in a valley hemmed in by steep grassy knolls.

The post had been established fifteen years ago, originally garrisoned by two companies of cavalry—three hundred men. Until recently, their job had been to protect the Nez Percé Indians from the encroachment of settlers and miners—a job performed with indifferent success. The fort boasted comfortable quarters for officers and enlisted men, as well as a school, a garden, parade ground, and laundry. Under normal circumstances a pleasant enough posting, thought Wettermark, when compared to some of the frontier forts he had seen. But circumstances were no longer normal, and Fort Lapwei was no longer an obscure outpost. In fact, engravings of the fort had recently appeared in *Harper's Weekly*. All eyes were on Fort Lapwei these days, for it stood directly in the eye of a hurricane of violence.

There were more than two companies here now—in fact, the parade ground and a clearing between the fort proper and the willow-lined creek were covered with tents, neat rows of white, canvas triangles. War was about to break out between the United States of America and the Nez Percé nation, and Fort Lapwei had been reinforced.

"My orders are to report directly to General Howard," Wettermark told the sentry at the gate.

"Yes, sir, Major. That's the officer of the day coming over now, sir. He will escort you to the general."

Moments later Wettermark was escorted into the office of Oliver Otis Howard, a man he had heard a lot about, but never met before today.

Howard had been awarded the Congressional Medal of Honor during the Civil War. After the war, he was put in charge of the Freedmen's Bureau, which was designed to assist in the enfranchisement of freed slaves in the South. A political post, and most military men would have been ill suited for the task. Howard, however, had an understanding of politics. Unfortunately, the individuals he selected to operate the Bureau had proven to be exceedingly corrupt, and the general's otherwise impeccable record carried the blemish of that affair to this day. By all accounts, Howard's bravery and intelligence and leadership ability were unquestioned, but the business with the Freedmen's Bureau indicated that in judgment he might be lacking.

Physically he was an imposing figure, tall and solidly built, with a piercing gaze and a full, rust-colored beard. The right sleeve of his tunic was empty, pinned to the red sash which girded his trim waist. The Indians called him One Hand. He lost the arm in one of the many battles he had fought in the Civil War, first as a regimental, then divisional, and finally corps commander.

Howard was standing before a wall map when Wettermark entered and introduced himself. "Very glad to have you assigned as my adjutant, Major," he said in a gravelly voice. "You have distinguished yourself in campaigns against the Sioux and the Northern Cheyenne. I am told you are quite well informed on the subject of the Plains Indian. You were born out here, were you not?"

"Yes, sir."

"What do you know about the Nez Percé? Or perhaps I should say, about our current difficulties with the Nez Percé."

Wettermark took a deep breath. "General, you specifically requested that I be attached to your staff, and you know everything there is to know about my record of service, I am sure. But are you aware of my reputation for being forthright?"

A smile moved the thick mat of red hair on Howard's lower face. "Indeed I do. It has gotten you into some hot water in the past, has it not?"

"Yes, sir."

"And you have not learned your lesson?"

"Yes, sir, I have. I learned it a long time ago, during the war, when I served under an officer who was conspicuously lacking in military training, not to mention common sense. A number of soldiers, good men, lost their lives as a direct result of that officer's ignorance and callous disregard for the welfare of his troops, and I stood by and kept my mouth shut and let it happen. I will not do that again."

Howard nodded. "Good. As a matter of fact, I have been informed of your knack for being brutally honest.

That's what I want from you. Candid assessments. And they had damned well be accurate ones, too."

"Yes, sir." Wettermark was pleased. "As for the Nez Percé, they are a singularly proud and honorable people, who have made every effort to remain on friendly terms with us. They have been provoked on countless occasions, and yet they remain obstinately committed to peace. If they have gone to war against us now, I can only say that they must have had good reason to do so."

Howard scowled at the map. "Well, if it looks, smells, and sounds like war, then it must be war. War parties have attacked wagons, isolated farms, a mining camp, even one of our patrols, all in the past week. There have been some atrocities, I believe, committed by warriors drunk on liquor. The settlers in the vicinity of Grangeville and Lewiston have taken flight. Many of them have sought protection under our wing right here at Fort Lapwei. The civilians would have me believe that the so-called nontreaty Indians are nothing but troublemakers, and that Chief Joseph is the worst of the lot. What do you think about that?"

"I have heard a lot about Chief Joseph," said Wettermark. "He is not a treacherous or warlike man."

"Perhaps not. But my job is to make certain this uprising is swiftly quelled. This kind of thing can be contagious, highly so, and we don't want it to spread to all the other tribes in the Northwest, do we? I have sent Captain Perry out with two troops, a hundred men, and eleven friendly Nez Percé to act as guides and interpreters. Captain Perry's orders are to put a stop to the raids, to protect the settlers. Reinforcements are on their way from Walla Walla. But I don't really think we will need those reinforcements, Major. I think we will make short work of this. Something on your mind?"

"I was just thinking, if we had done a better job of protecting the Nez Percé from the settlers, we wouldn't have to be protecting the settlers from the Nez Percé now."

"Would you care to elaborate?"

"Yes, sir. Thank you, I would. We gave the Nez Percé this land in perpetuity back in 1855. We promised to keep our people out. For some reason, we failed to keep our promise. Then . . . "

Howard held up his hand.

"You are a principled and fair-minded man, Major. I appreciate that. But it is irrelevant. As of the executive order from President Grant on June 10, 1875, the Nez Percé were directed to leave this reservation and proceed to the new allotment along the . . . "

"A coyote couldn't live on the land we're giving them," said Wettermark, and added, "sir."

"We are soldiers, Major Wettermark. We must obey orders."

"Yes, sir. What are my orders, General?"

"Tomorrow a detachment will be leaving to reinforce Captain Perry. I want you to go along. Assess the situation. Although you will outrank Perry, I do not intend that you take command of the force, unless, in your best judgment, it is absolutely necessary."

"Yes, sir." Wettermark was relieved. This was one command he did not want.

"That is all," said Howard, and turned back to the map, missing Wettermark's snappy salute.

Outside, Wettermark led his weary horse across the crowded parade ground in the direction of the stables. A cavalryman through and through, he always took care of his mount before attending to his own needs. But, unlike many other officers, he never left it to a subordinate. He would feed, water, and brush out the sorrel himself. Having been born and reared on the plains, he knew that to be afoot was, in most cases, certain death out here, and for this reason he trusted no one else with the care of his cayuse.

"Major!"

Wettermark turned to see a stocky man wearing a brown tweed suit, derby hat, and prodigious side whiskers hurrying to catch up with him.

"Major Wettermark. I had heard you were coming to Fort Lapwei. Do you remember me?"

"We've met before, I know, but . . . "

"Zebulon Bigelow, correspondent for the *Baltimore Sun*."

"Oh yes. The campaign against the Northern Cheyenne."

"Quite right!" Bigelow beamed, fished a "short six" cigar from his jacket pocket. "Care for a smoke, Major?"

"No, thanks. What are you doing here, Mr. Bigelow?"

"Another Indian war." Bigelow shrugged expansively. "Either they like my work or they just don't want me back in Baltimore. I haven't been home in four years."

"At least you have a home."

"Referring to yourself, Major?"

Wettermark shook his head. He had been thinking about the Nez Percé.

"I was hoping you could tell me what is happening," said Bigelow.

"As you said, another Indian war."

"All I get from the other officers is that the Nez Percé are on the warpath. But you and I both know there are always two sides to every story. Are you aware that there is growing sympathy for the plight of the Indian back east? You are an acknowledged expert on the tribes of the Great Plains. What has provoked the peace-loving Nez Percé to take up their weapons against us?"

Wettermark glanced across the sun-hammered, dust-choked parade ground at the headquarters building. He knew General Howard would frown on his talking candidly with a correspondent. Yet, in his opinion, the Nez Percé were getting the short end of the stick, and that irked him.

"Anything you can tell me would, of course, be strictly confidential," added Bigelow, seeing that Wettermark wavered. "And I am not inquiring after details of the campaign you intend to embark upon. I'm just curious to know more about the Nez Percé. They have always been our friends, haven't they?"

"But we've never been theirs," said Wettermark. "You want to know what's happening, Mr. Bigelow? I'll tell you. The Nez Percé are in the way, and our orders are to move them."

"In the way of what?"

"Progress."

"You don't sound convinced that it is for the best."

"For the best or not, it's inevitable," said Wettermark. "Look, at the Council of 1855 we promised the Nez Percé they could keep their homeland forever. Then the miners moved in, and instead of throwing them out, which we should have done, we bought seven million acres at eight cents an acre, leaving the Indians with less than a quarter of the land guaranteed them in 1855. Eight cents an acre, Mr. Bigelow. Don't you wish you could buy an acre of land so cheaply. Problem with that sale is that only a handful of the Nez Percé headmen made their mark to it. Chief Joseph's band, and others, continued to live on their land, even though it had been sold out from under them. Needless to say, there was trouble. Our own people didn't pay any attention to the new agreement, either. When they found land they liked they took it, regardless of who it belonged to. We took the best grazing lands, the best timber, and the best water. Little wonder that for a dozen years we've had some scrapes with the Nez Percé.

They're finally fed up. This order by the president, to take what's left of their land and move them off, has done the trick."

"But not all the bands are on the warpath, are they?"

"Not yet," said Wettermark. "Just the Wallowa band—Chief Joseph's. But General Howard is right about one thing. If we don't nip this in the bud it will only get worse."

"I've heard that Howard is sympathetic towards the Indians," said Bigelow, rolling the cigar around in his mouth.

Wettermark nodded. "As Commandant of the Department of the Columbia he reviewed the situation a couple of years ago. Sent his adjutant general to study the matter. The adjutant general reported that in his opinion the nontreaty Nez Percé—the ones who never signed an agreement with the United States—could not be regarded in law as bound by the treaty. General Howard informed the War Department that he believed it to be a great mistake to attempt to drive Joseph and his people from the Wallowa, and recommended we leave them in peace."

"Apparently it didn't do any good."

"None whatsoever. And don't misjudge the general, Mr. Bigelow. He will do his duty."

"As I am confident you will do yours, Major. I'm wondering if I could accompany you into the field."

"You'll have to get General Howard's permission," said Wettermark, and by his tone of voice it was obvious he did not think Bigelow had a chance of getting any such thing from old One Hand.

"I'll do that," said Bigelow, with a cheery and indefatigable smile. "I'll be seeing you, Captain."

Wettermark turned away.

"Oh, Major."

"Yes?"

"Have you heard of the Gray Warrior?"

"Can't say that I have."

"I've talked to a couple of traders, and a missionary by the name of Williams. They say there is a white man living near the Wallowa. An ex-Confederate soldier, married to an Indian woman. On occasion, according to these sources, he has fought alongside the Nez Percé. Never against other whites, mind you. Just other Indians— Shoshone, Bannock. No one knows his true identity, although he has by all accounts lived here in this country for at least ten years."

"No," said Wettermark. "That's the first I've heard of this man."

Brows knit, he watched Bigelow walk away. Something nagged at the back of his mind regarding this tale of an ex-Confederate living among the Nez Percé— something he couldn't quite put a finger on.

16

Dalton's arrival at the camp of the nontreaty Nez Percé was cause for great rejoicing among the Indians. Scouts brought word in advance of his coming, and a dozen young braves rode out to greet him. With him rode Turns from the Light. She led a single pack horse. The braves circled them, their shouts of approbation piercing the hot, still afternoon.

As he entered the camp—thirty to forty lodges beneath the trees which lined White Bird Creek—Dalton was quick to notice that most of the warriors were absent. There were women and children, young men and old. But the men with whom he had on occasion gone to war, against the Shoshone and the Bannock and the Blackfeet, were not here. Conspicuous by his absence was Ollokot, Chief Joseph's brother, and the most renowned fighter in the Wallowa band.

But Chief Joseph was present. Tall, broad shouldered, head held high with that *simiakin*—the fierce Nez Percé pride—etched into features so stern and immobile that they seemed carved from Idaho granite. He was a man of tremendous presence, possessed of *wyakin*, an undeniable ability to lead other men.

Dalton was glad to see Toohoolzote standing beside Chief Joseph. Dismounting Indian-style, he embraced his old friend the song singer. It struck him that in the twelve years he had known Toohoolzote the Indian had scarcely changed at all. He was still slender and boyishly young in his looks. But Toohoolzote had changed in some ways. He was not of the Wallowa band, but had joined Chief Joseph in protest of the treaty which had robbed his people of their land. He was not the only one to have done so.

"You're a sight for sore eyes, Toohoolzote," said Dalton. "I was surprised to hear you had joined the Wallowas."

"You were right, Graycoat. We should have fought them a long time ago. I am still not much of a fighter, but perhaps Coyote will hear my songs and guide us to victory."

"Graycoat," said Joseph, "it is good that you have come."

"You have allowed me to live on your land for twelve years." Dalton glanced at Light, still astride her paint pony. She smiled at him, and he marvelled—as he did every time he saw her—at her beauty. She was truly *palo-jami*—a fair one. "They have been the best years of my life. But I knew they could not last forever."

"You still want to fight the bluecoats, my friend?" asked Toohoolzote. "Do you still hate them?"

"I don't know that I hate them anymore, Song Singer, but I will fight them. Not because of what they have done to me, but because of what they are doing to my friends, the Nez Percé."

Joseph extended his hand. Dalton clasped it tightly. The women, children, and young braves who were present to see this gave a shout.

"The people know we have never lost a fight when Graycoat rode with us," said Joseph.

Toohoolzote, noting that Dalton was clad in buckskins, asked him if he had brought the tunic of butternut-gray.

The gray tunic, he said, was powerful medicine. Dalton went to his horse, a mouse-colored mustang, and untied the blanket rolled up behind the cantle of his saddle. The tunic was inside the blanket. He held it up for the Nez Percé to see, and another great shout rose up.

"Come," said Joseph, turning to enter his lodge. "We will share a pipe and talk."

Sitting cross-legged on elk skins, Joseph, Dalton and the song singer passed the pipe around. No one spoke until everyone had smoked. In the privacy of his lodge Joseph dropped the stony mask and allowed his expression to reflect his deep concern.

"My scouts tell me the soldiers are coming," he informed Dalton. "They may be here by nightfall."

"How many?"

"At least a hundred. I have sent Ollokot and Yellow Wolf and most of the warriors to watch them."

"How many warriors do you have, Joseph?"

"No more than eighty. But only half possess guns, and most of those are muzzle-loading muskets acquired from the fur traders. The soldiers have rifles which shoot many times without reloading."

"And ammunition is scarce," added Toohoolzote.

"This valley is not a good place to fight," warned Dalton. "You should move your people up into the mountains."

"Our women have been gathering the camas," said Joseph, "and our young men have been bringing in the horses and the cattle."

Dalton nodded. Camas Prairie was a few miles north of here. Joseph knew that with war coming there would be no time for hunting and fishing, and he was wise to have the women hard at work collecting the bulbs of the blue lily, available now that the summer sun had evaporated the shallow waters of the marshy camas fields. The bulbs were steamed by the bushel over heated stones while covered with wet meadow grass—Dalton had seen this being done as he entered the village—then mashed and shaped into loaves and baked. Joseph realized that he would need a good supply of this nourishing Indian bread.

"What is your plan?" asked Dalton.

"We will cross the Bitterroots on the Lolo Trail and seek sanctuary among the Crows."

"You are going to leave your land?" Dalton was surprised.

"The *Shoyapee* have taken our land. There are too many of them, and too few of us. I have never been for war, Graycoat. I know too many of the white people who live here. Some of them are good friends. I have shared their food. I have hunted with the men. I have honored their women, and loved their children, as I love Nez Percé children. In a war it is not just the men who die. The bullet finds the woman and the child, too.

"I have always been for peace. But some of our young, hotheaded warriors got drunk on whiskey and killed some white people. I knew then that we would have to leave. The soldiers are coming to kill us. We must go. But we will not go on their reservation. We will go east instead, across the mountains, to join our friends the Crows, with whom we have always hunted the buffalo.

"I will not go to the reservation because they want to take our children and put them in their schools and teach them to be Nez Percé no longer. Do you understand, Graycoat? They have stolen the land, but they will not steal our children. The Nez Percé will remain Nez Percé as long as I am alive."

"I do understand," said Dalton. "That's why, after the war, I did not go home, but instead came here. I knew my home would not be the same. The Yankees were determined to change the way we lived, and I would not put myself beneath the heel of a tyrant."

Joseph nodded. "Other bands will join us. The Salmon River, the Palouse, the Asotin, the White Bird . . . "

Frowning, Dalton shook his head.

"What is it, Graycoat?" asked Toohoolzote. "What is wrong?"

"Couple of things. One, I don't much care for retreat. And that's what you're planning to do. They won't just let you go. They won't understand your motives, Joseph. They call you a malcontent. A dangerous Indian. They'll send the whole army after you. Even if you make it to Crow country, do you think they will leave you alone?" Dalton shook his head. "They won't."

"Then we will go to Canada," said Joseph grimly. "But it is too late to stand and fight. All my people would die."

"If you went deep and high into the mountains, you could hold out there for years."

"What good would that do?"

"I've heard folks back east have started to change their minds about the way the army's been treating the tribes out here."

"You do not have to come with us, Graycoat. I can make no one go with me if they do not wish to."

"I'll go. It'll be a running fight, and maybe I can do you some good."

Dalton didn't tell Joseph and Toohoolzote what he was most afraid of—that this retreat would end up just like the one he had participated in twelve years ago, when the Army of Northern Virginia abandoned Richmond and fled west, hounded by Grant and the Army of the Potomac.

"My heart is happy to hear these words," said Joseph. "Our young warriors know we have never lost in battle when you rode with them wearing the gray coat."

"Besides," added Toohoolzote, "we have never fought

the yellowlegs before. You have. Perhaps you will be able to tell us what they will do next."

"I'll do my best. Right now I'd like to go join Ollokot and Yellow Wolf."

Joseph nodded.

Dalton turned to Toohoolzote. "You will look after Light until I return?"

The song singer promised he would.

The eastern sky was gray tinged with pink when the soldiers reached the canyon of the White Bird. From atop a butte with Yellow Wolf and three other warriors Dalton watched them. There were only eleven in the party—eight soldiers, two friendly Nez Percé scouts, and a civilian Yellow Wolf was able to identify as Narrow Eyes Chapman. Even at this great distance Yellow Wolf was certain. He recognized Chapman's horse, a palomino. Chapman was well known among the Nez Percé. He was a rabid Indian hater. Yellow Wolf's contempt for Chapman was exceeded only by that which he reserved for the Nez Percé scouts who were serving the United States Army, traitors to their own people. It was bad enough, declared Yellow Wolf, that so many Nez Percé were submitting meekly to the tyrannical demands of the *Shoyapee* and going to the new reservation. But to betray their own people as these scouts were doing . . . It was all Yellow Wolf could do to refrain from charging down there on his war pony with rifle blazing to snuff out their worthless lives.

"The rest of the yellowlegs wait behind the hill," he said. "Why do they send only these few into the valley, Graycoat?"

"I reckon their commander is afraid of walking into a trap," replied Dalton.

He looked west, at a tree-cloaked ridge beyond a creek, where he knew Ollokot and fifty Nez Percé warriors were waiting. There was absolutely nothing to indicate that so much as a single Indian lurked in those woods, but Dalton had complete confidence in Ollokot. Joseph's brother was a man who could be relied upon to be where he said he was going to be.

Dalton turned his attention to the valley. He could not see the village, because it was hidden behind a shoulder of the butte, but he noticed the gray pall of woodsmoke from the morning lodge fires hanging in the still air of a summer dawn.

"We'd better send another rider to Joseph," he told Yellow Wolf.

Yellow Wolf nodded. He told one of the warriors to ride to Joseph and inform him of the arrival of the soldiers. They had dispatched a rider last night to warn the village that the yellowlegs would reach the White Bird by daybreak. Dalton wondered why the village was so quiet. Joseph could not have already left the valley with all his people. There simply hadn't been enough time for a full-scale evacuation. So what was he doing?

The eleven-man advance party had reached a draw which would take them down to the floor of the valley. Dalton figured they were hardly more than a mile from the village now. A moment later several Indians appeared at the mouth of the draw. They had come from the village. One of them carried a white flag.

"Damn," muttered Dalton.

"What is Joseph doing?" asked Yellow Dog, shocked and angry.

"We'd better find out."

They were turning their horses when a shot rang out. Then another.

The light was better now, and Dalton could clearly see the rifle at the shoulder of the man named Chapman. The Indians under the white flag were racing away, back towards the village. One rode slumped forward, and another was trying to keep his galloping pony alongside so that he could hold his wounded friend up on his horse.

"That bastard," rasped Dalton, the rage surging inside him. He pulled the fringed elk skin sheath—the one Light had made for him—from the barrel of the Hawken buffalo gun, intending to take a crack at Chapman. The distance, a quarter-mile, was well within the range of the .50 caliber rifle.

But before he could get off a shot one of the Indians hidden in the trees fired first—and one of the soldiers toppled backwards off his horse.

In the next instant Ollokot and his warriors were pouring out of the woods, shooting and yelling as their ponies splashed across the creek. The advance party of soldiers dismounted. A bugle sounded from the far side of the hill.

Yellow Wolf and the other two warriors with Dalton threw their blankets to the ground. They were stripped for battle, wearing only loincloths, moccasins, paint, and war charms.

"Let's go," said Dalton, that old familiar tingle, that thrill of battle, shooting through him like lightning. He kicked his horse into a headlong gallop down the steep slope, the Nez Percé warriors on his heels, a war cry on their lips.

17

After the fight, Dalton could point to Captain Perry's decision to dismount his men at the crest of the hill and adopt a defensive posture instead of charging to the rescue of the advance guard as the decisive factor. Had Perry been more aggressive he might well have made short work of the Nez Percé War. Instead, he was too worried about leading his command into a trap. Dalton figured this timidity had something to do with the recent disaster suffered by the Army at Little Bighorn, where the Seventh Cavalry had been all but wiped out by the Sioux under Crazy Horse.

This sealed the fate of the advance guard, commanded by a lieutenant named Theller. Ollokot and his warriors were upon them in a blink of an eye. A few, among these the Nez Percé scouts and the civilian, Narrow Eyes Chapman, turned and fled. Theller and his soldiers stood their ground and were overwhelmed by an Indian tide. Before Dalton and Yellow Wolf could reach the draw it was finished. The lieutenant and his men lay dead.

A brief lull followed. The Nez Percé had killed some yellowlegs, and many of them were willing to let it go at that. But not Ollokot. Dalton took one look at Joseph's brother and saw the fire in his eyes. Ollokot was consumed by a blood lust. He wanted to charge straight up the hill into the soldiers lining up on the crest. Dalton talked some sense into him. He had studied the lay of the land, and knew that if they kept to the draw it would lead them to an outcropping of rocks on Perry's flank. Perry had posted a dozen or so civilian volunteers among the rocks, thinking they would have no trouble anchoring that end of his line. Dalton had been in too many battles not to notice this, and he had a hunch Perry was overestimating the fighting ability of the civilians.

His hunch proved right. The Nez Percé warriors followed him up the draw and into the rocks, and they were sheltered most of the way from the guns of the cavalrymen along the crest. When the Indians reached the outcropping the civilians turned and fled. The warriors wanted to give chase, but Dalton managed to get most of them to turn and plunge into the bluecoat line.

More than a dozen troopers fell in the brief but bloody melée that followed. Dalton accounted for two of them on his own, using the Schofield now. A cavalryman appeared suddenly out of the choking drift of dust and powdersmoke, grabbing for Dalton, trying to drag him out of the saddle. Dalton shot him at point-blank range. The soldier's face dissolved into a scarlet mask. As the troopers broke and ran for their horses, Dalton turned after them. A horse tender took a shot at him and missed. Dalton fired back, and didn't miss. The horses the dead man had been holding scattered, leaving several of the soldiers without mounts and easy prey.

Then, abruptly, it was over, and the broken remnants of Perry's command were streaming to the north in full, panicked retreat, leaving over thirty soldiers dead on the slopes of White Bird Canyon. A number of warriors gave chase. This time Dalton could not stop them.

To everyone's amazement, not a single Nez Percé had lost his life. Three had been wounded, including the man Chapman had shot to start the action. Over sixty repeating rifles and a number of pistols were retrieved. The dead soldiers were searched for ammunition. Dalton was glad to see that the Nez Percé did not mutilate the corpses. He had heard that some Indians were notorious for that kind of grisly work.

Dalton accompanied Ollokot and Yellow Wolf and the other warriors back to the village. Ollokot proclaimed a great victory, and there was much rejoicing. But Toohoolzote noticed Dalton's grave expression.

"Why the long face, Graycoat?" asked the song singer. "Is this not a great day for the Nez Percé? Is this not what you have always said we should do?"

"When I fought with General Lee we won many battles," said Dalton. "But still we lost the war. We whipped a hundred soldiers today, Toohoolzote. Next time there might be a thousand."

That night, in the skin lodge which had been erected for them, Dalton made love to Turns from the Light, but even so, Light could tell he was preoccupied. When she woke in the early morning hours she found him sitting outside the lodge, smoking his pipe, and staring off into space with a frown fixed on his face. She knelt behind him and wrapped her arms around him, whispered sweet nothings in his ear, and yet she could not entice him back to their bed of buffalo robes.

"I'm sorry," he said, "but I must go talk to Joseph." And he abruptly left her.

He found Joseph standing in front of his own lodge, wrapped in a scarlet blanket and gazing at the stars. The village was quiet. The celebration had finally exhausted itself. The fires around which the victorious warriors had danced and recounted their daring exploits had died down to orange embers glowing in mounds of gray ash. Dalton had not taken part in the festivities.

"You are troubled, Graycoat."

"Why the white flag, Joseph?"

"I hoped to reason with the yellowlegs."

"Too late for that. You saw what happened."

Joseph nodded sadly.

"I realize that you hate war," said Dalton, "but war is exactly what you've got. You must either fight or go to the reservation. Make up your mind, Joseph."

He wasn't sure how Joseph would take to being spoken to in such a manner, but the Nez Percé leader merely smiled tolerantly.

"The decision has been made for me now, wouldn't you say?"

Dalton nodded. "Yes, I guess it has."

"What will One Hand do now?"

Dalton knew that Joseph was referring to General O. O. Howard.

"He'll come himself next time, with many more men."

"How long?"

"We ought to be on the move by tomorrow, next day at the very latest."

"It is very sad," reflected Joseph, again looking up at the stars, "to leave the land where you were born, the land nourished by the blood of your forefathers. But we will go."

"Joseph, that man named Chapman fired the first shot, it's true. But thirty-three soldiers died yesterday. They'll call it a massacre. There will be no quarter given now. Hell, they might even put a price on your head."

"And yours, Graycoat."

Dalton smiled. "Then I guess we'd better not get caught."

•　　　•　　　•

The detachment which Major Wettermark accompanied did not join up with Captain Perry until after the Battle of White Bird Canyon. All Wettermark could do was ride back to Fort Lapwei with the beaten remnants of Perry's command. He listened carefully to all the talk about the fight, and once back at the outpost, made his assessment to General Howard.

His report contradicted Perry's in several ways. While Perry insisted that the white flag had been part of a diabolical plot on the part of the Indians to lure his men into a trap, Wettermark was inclined to believe, given the past history of the tribe, not to mention Joseph's well-known proclivities, that it had been a genuine attempt to avoid bloodshed. And while Perry defended his decision to form a defensive line on the hilltop, Wettermark offered his studied opinion that by doing so Perry had abandoned Lieutenant Theller and the advance guard to their fate. They both concurred that the presence of civilians had only made matters worse.

Howard was inclined to believe Wettermark, but he told the major he could not take official action against Perry based solely on the opinion of an officer who had not even been present in the field of battle. None of Perry's subordinates would corroborate Wettermark's version of the battle. That didn't surprise him. He was the outsider, not Perry.

Several days later Howard left Fort Lapwei with several hundred troops from the First Cavalry and the Twenty-first Infantry, as well as packers, guides, a mountain howitzern, and two Gatling guns. There were also twenty civilian volunteers from Walla Walla. Wettermark knew Howard didn't want those men along, but there they were just the same, and Wettermark figured it had something to do with the politics of the situation. Howard was always keenly aware of the politics.

Zebulon Bigelow was also present. Howard had not

given him permission to join Perry's command, but apparently the correspondent had persuaded the general to change his mind. Wettermark was glad. He had a hunch Bigelow would tell both sides of this tragic tale. If General Howard thought he could manipulate Bigelow into regurgitating the official line, Wettermark was confident the correspondent would soon disabuse him of that mistaken notion.

Reports from the survivors of the Battle of White Bird Canyon about a white man in Confederate uniform riding with the Nez Percé warriors kept nagging at Wettermark's mind. He was inclined to think it must have been an Indian who had somehow acquired a tunic of Rebel gray. But some of the troopers insisted that the man they'd seen was white. Wettermark recalled leading a patrol twelve years ago in pursuit of a Confederate officer who had killed several soldiers in a shootout in Franklin, Missouri. They had lost the Rebel's trail on the sagebrush flats of eastern Colorado. Could it be possible . . . ? Wettermark decided it wasn't likely.

While sitting around a campfire one night, Bigelow asked Wettermark about the Confederate renegade.

"I've been told by one of the civilians that some of the Nez Percé scouts have spoken of a man called Graycoat," said the correspondent, mumbling over a big stogie clenched in his teeth. "They say this man has been living among the Indians for more than ten years."

"You do have a way of finding out things, don't you, Mr. Bigelow?"

Pleased, Bigelow chuckled. "It's my job. I keep wondering about that man, though. You know, I made the acquaintance of a Confederate officer in West Virginia at the end of the war. Lee had surrendered, and this officer was traveling west with a young woman, his wife . . . Have I said something, Major?"

"This woman. Can you describe her?"

"Very attractive, as I recall. Early twenties. Chestnut-brown hair. I don't remember her name. But I think his was Dalton. Forgive me for saying so, Major, but you've just turned as white as a boiled shirt."

"That same summer a woman fitting that description arrived in Franklin, Missouri, with a Confederate officer."

"I saw them both off on a train bound for St. Louis."

"The woman was killed in a shootout between that officer and several soldiers."

"What happened to the officer?"

Wettermark told him.

Bigelow was thoughtfully silent for a moment, digesting this news. He produced a silver flask from his tweed jacket and took a swig before offering it to Wettermark.

"It is indeed a small world, isn't it, Major?"

Wettermark accepted the flask and took pleasure in discovering that it contained very smooth Tennessee sour mash. "It is indeed, Mr. Bigelow."

"I wonder . . ." said Bigelow.

He didn't need to finish. Wettermark nodded. "So do I."

18

Five days after the battle in White Bird Canyon, news reached the Nez Percé village that One Hand Howard was coming.

It had been an anxious five days for Dalton. He couldn't believe the Indians were not already on their way to Crow country. It was through no fault of Chief Joseph's. The headman had tried repeatedly to talk some sense into his people. But they would not listen. A strange thing had happened to them—or at least it seemed strange to Joseph. The people were in the grip of an odd kind of lethargy. They had whipped the yellowlegs, who by now must be afraid of the Nez Percé. The *Shoyapee* had been taught a lesson, and they would surely not be so foolish as to bother the Nez Percé anymore. This nonsense seemed to be the consensus among the people. And why should they listen to Joseph anyway? He had not been in the big fight. No, Joseph had stayed in the village, safe and sound, along with the women and the children.

Their attitude did not surprise Dalton. The Nez Percé had won a battle, and now they were feeling cocky. The same thing had happened to the Confederacy in the aftermath of the First Battle at Bull Run, when the Federals had been thoroughly chastised and routed. Dalton remembered the subsequent talk. Many had assumed the Yankees would sue for peace. Of course, it hadn't taken too long for them to learn otherwise.

Only when the scouts came in with the news of Howard's coming did the Nez Percé begin to get nervous. The decision was made to move up the Salmon River at least as far as Horseshoe Bend. That was better than nothing, thought Dalton. White Bird Canyon was no place to be caught by the army—a fact Perry would have demonstrated had he not been such a gold-plated fool.

And so it began.

Howard was soon hot on their heels, pausing only long enough to give the thirty-three dead soldiers in White Bird Canyon a decent burial. The Indians got across the Salmon just before hard rains came and made the river jump its banks. They were slowed somewhat on account of the vast horse herd which they had resolved would not be left behind for the avaricious whites. The hope was that the high-running river would stop One Hand, but Howard managed to get some of his troopers across. There was growing panic among the Nez Percé then, but with the help of Ollokot and Yellow Wolf, Dalton got the council to agree to a plan. While the main body of Indians continued on the move, Dalton and Yellow Wolf and a dozen warriors would lead the cavalrymen on a merry chase.

This was rough country, deep ravines and high ridges and many creeks now raging out of control due to the persistent rains, and before long the soldiers were exhausted. Dalton had fought with the Nez Percé warriors before, and knew they could outlast the yellowlegs. He had heard that the whites called them "half wolf, half horse, and half otter," and they proved why as they spent days leading the soldiers on a wild goose chase. Not once did the bluecoats get close enough to engage them in a fight, and all the while the main body of the Nez Percé got further and further away.

Howard tried his utmost to get the rest of his command across the raging river. But when he finally succeeded in doing so he discovered it was all for naught. The Nez Percé, well ahead of him now, had recrossed the river at Craig Billy Crossing, at the mouth of Captain Billy Creek. By doing so the Indians threatened the white settlement of Lewiston—in fact they were between Howard and the town. The Indians had crossed the river by making bullboats out of pack covers and willow branches, and their horses seemed to swim as strongly as they ran. Howard could not get across. He had no choice but to backtrack to White Bird Crossing.

Meanwhile the Nez Percé struck out across Camas Prairie, making for the Lolo Trail, which would take them across the Bitterroots into Montana. They were surprised to find a detachment of soldiers at Camas Prairie. These troops, commanded by Captain Stephen Whipple, were dug in at Cottonwood House, a stage station. Whipple sent ten troopers and two civilian guides out to ascertain the strength and disposition of the Indians. All twelve men perished in an ambush by warriors under the inspired leadership of Rainbow and Five Wounds. The Nez Percé were so encouraged that they went so far as to attack Cottonwood House, but, on Dalton's advice, Joseph called them off. Dalton surmised that Whipple would be too shaken to make an aggressive move any time soon, and he was right. The yellowlegs remained dug in at Cottonwood House while the Nez Percé moved on to the South Fork of the Clearwater.

Here Joseph's people were joined by the bands of Looking Glass and Husis Kute, which included a number of Palouses. To Dalton's consternation, the Indians lingered on the banks of the Clearwater. They were in high spirits. They had outwitted One Hand. Surely now they were safe.

When Ben Wettermark answered General Howard's summons he braced himself for a bad experience. Howard was in his tent, in the middle of the army's bivouac on the outskirts of the town called Grangeville. He was bent over a wooden folding table, working on a report by the light of a kerosene lantern. When Wettermark came through the tent flap he did not even look up, but rather kept writing as he spoke.

"I'm catching pure hell, Major."

"Yes, sir. I know."

"They're saying I let Joseph escape. They're saying he outwitted me. That he is some kind of military genius. In fact, one particular newspaperman has dubbed him the 'Indian Napoleon.'" Now Howard looked up, and his gaze was icy. "Do you know which newspaperman I mean?"

"Yes, sir. Zebulon Bigelow."

"You two have become friends?"

"Not friends," said Wettermark. "No, I wouldn't go that far. But he tries to write the truth, and I respect him for it."

"Whose truth?"

"There is only one truth, General."

"Where did he get this Indian Napoleon nonsense? From you?"

"No, sir. In fact, he's wrong on that score. I doubt that Joseph has had much to do with their success, frankly. Joseph, as headman of the Wallowa band, participates in the council, but he does not make any decision alone. To be honest, I think his brother, Ollokot, is the war leader of the Nez Percé."

"Ollokot. Well, he has made a mistake."

"How so?"

"The nontreaties are encamped on the South Fork of the Clearwater. Have been for several days. A few other bands have joined them there. Reports now put their number at about eight hundred souls."

"Which means probably two hundred fighting men."

Howard nodded. "Fifty civilians led by Ed McConville are the ones who have located them. McConville is hiding out nearby, waiting for the army to get there. We will be underway an hour before sunrise. With any luck we will catch the hostiles between us and McConville."

The evening of the day that Wettermark met with General Howard, a council was held in the Nez Percé camp among the trees on the banks of the Clearwater's south fork. Joseph was there, as were Ollokot and Yellow Wolf, Looking Glass, Husis Kute, Rainbow, and Five Wounds. Dalton was present as well, with Toohoolzote standing by to serve as his interpreter, even though in twelve years Dalton had acquired a fair grasp of the Indian tongue, enough to get him through in most circumstances.

This was the first time Dalton had been invited to sit in at a council meeting, and he was glad for the opportunity, because this lingering on the Clearwater deeply troubled him, and he hoped to be able to speak his piece and persuade the Indians of their peril. However, as a guest, he could not speak unless given express permission to do so by one of the council members. He wondered who had invited him in the first place, and to what purpose. Might it have been Joseph?

Joseph's attitude puzzled Dalton. For almost an hour he sat quietly as the conversation swirled around him. He looked grim, almost angry.

For a long while the talk centered on the group of civilians which had been discovered encamped on Mount Idaho not far to the north. They had been driven further away, and a number of warriors led by Two Moons was still harassing them.

Looking Glass explained why he had joined the renegades. "I have always lived in peace with the white man. Even so, my village was attacked by the yellowlegs. I tried to surrender, even though I was not at war. But it did no good. The soldiers stole our food and our livestock. I complained to the agent. He laughed in my face. The chief of the yellowlegs who attacked my village said it was all a big mistake. I asked for our food and our livestock to be returned to us. I was told it would take a little while for these things to be returned." The expression on the old Asotin headman's creased and leathery face was bitter. Anger blazed in his rheumy eyes. "They think I am *meopkowit*, an old fool. I know now these things will never be given back to us. The white man is a lying, thieving dog. *Kiuala piyakasiusa*. It is time to fight. I say we attack the yellowlegs holed up in Cottonwood House."

"I agree with Looking Glass," said Yellow Wolf. "We do not have to cross the mountains into Crow country. Why should our women and children and old people suffer the rigors of the Lolo Trail? Every time we fight the *Shoyapee* they turn and run away. We have killed almost fifty of them, and not a single warrior has lost his life. We used to be afraid because we knew there were so many soldiers who could march against us. But now we know that ten Nez Percé warriors can prevail against a hundred yellowlegs. What do we have to worry about?"

Dalton glanced across the council fire at Joseph. Joseph was watching him, and Dalton could not fathom his expression. He wondered why Joseph wasn't challenging this dangerous overconfidence. Perhaps he was just tired of issuing warnings which his people, in their hubris, refused to heed.

"We cannot attack Cottonwood House while the whites with McConville are still near," reasoned Ollokot. "I know McConville. He talks big, but he is not much of a fighter. And do not forget that McConville and some of his men are riding our own ponies that they stole from us. I say we go upriver and kill McConville and his men and take back our property."

"I think One Hand has given up," opined Five Wounds. "Maybe we can stay on our land after all. We should at least wait and see what happens."

Dalton shook his head. He turned to Toohoolzote. "I cannot sit still and listen to this foolish talk any longer," he said, and stood up.

His outburst shocked the council members. Toohoolzote paled, casting a wary eye in the direction of Five Wounds and Yellow Wolf, the two warriors present whom he considered the most volatile. He was concerned for Dalton's welfare, because it would be out of character for either Five Wounds or Yellow Wolf to tolerate such incivility, even from the Gray Warrior.

It was Joseph, speaking for the first time since the council began, who broke the tension-laden silence.

"What would you have us do, Graycoat?"

"You told me once that you were glad to have me along because I could tell you what the soldiers would probably do. Well, I'm going to tell you, even though you're not going to like it. One Hand will never give up. I fought against him. I know him. He is not afraid of the Nez Percé. But you should be afraid of him. Three days we have lingered here. By now we could have been halfway across the Bitterroot Mountains. Thing is, you won't even be safe in Montana. I say go into the mountains. Make One Hand come after you. Find a strong defensive position and hold out as long as you can. Make the yellowlegs pay dearly in their blood for every foot of ground they have stolen from you. This camp is no good. It is a death trap. If you stay here you will find out it is so. No, hold out as long as you can in your mountain stronghold. If the cost in yellowleg lives is high, the people back east will sit up and take notice. It's conceivable they might listen to the Nez Percé side of things. It is a slim chance, I know, but it is also your only chance."

Yellow Wolf snorted in derision. "You could not beat the yellowlegs, Graycoat, you and your people. That is why you fear them. But then, you are not Nez Percé."

"Yellow Wolf is a great warrior. His trouble is, he thinks with his balls, not his brains."

Yellow Wolf shot to his feet and spat an obscenity. Dalton stood his ground. Toohoolzote noticed that he did not even flinch, and admired his friend for his courage.

Ollokot rose to Dalton's defense. "Graycoat is one of us," he told Yellow Wolf, with stern reproach. "He has fought beside us against the Shoshone and the Bannock and now the yellowlegs. He should be heard."

"I have spoken," said Dalton. Turning on his heel, he walked away.

His black mood dissipated somewhat when he reached his skin lodge and laid eyes on Light. She always had that effect on him, reminding him with just a glance and a shy smile that as long as he had her all the troubles of the world were actually of little consequence. When she heard what had transpired at the council she did a rare thing—she offered her opinion that they should leave the Nez Percé and go. Bid Joseph and Toohoolzote and Ollokot *taz alago* and ride for Canada. In Canada they would be safe.

Dalton was sorely tempted to do just that. He was tired of thinking about war. He longed to go somewhere

where he and Light could live in peace. But in the end he could not bring himself to desert the Nez Percé, not just yet.

Light did what she could to erase the frown from his face, luring him to the buffalo robes, and making him forget all about the council, and he went to sleep locked in the warm embrace of her arms and legs . . .

. . . And awoke the next morning to a sound from the past, a sound he knew only too well.

The boom of Yankee cannon.

19

In horror Dalton realized that Light was not in the skin lodge. Clad only in his leggings, he burst outside, into a scene of pandemonium. Men, women, and children were running in all directions, shouting or screaming or crying. He heard the all-too-familiar whiffling sound of shot in flight, and threw himself to the ground as an explosion a hundred feet away tossed rock and red earth skyward. Pouncing to his feet, he spared the mangled remains of two Nez Percé, a man and a woman, a brief glance. Then his dark and angry gaze swept the bluffs across the river, and he saw the white puff of powdersmoke, followed by another boom like thunder. This time the explosion tore a skin lodge apart.

Bastards, thought Dalton, with cold savagery. Firing artillery into a camp with no regard for the lives of women and children.

Yellow Wolf came running by. Dalton grabbed him by the arm.

"Where is Light?"

Yellow Wolf shook his head. He looked dazed. "What is happening, Graycoat?"

"One Hand's brought a howitzer along. Send some

men with rifles down to the river. Tell them to shoot at
the rim of the bluffs to keep the soldiers' heads down.
Get the women and children out of the camp and away
from the river."

Yellow Wolf nodded. Dalton's calm seemed to rub off
on him. Dalton refrained from asking the warrior if he
still thought One Hand was afraid of the Nez Percé, and
let him go.

His first concern was finding Light, and he turned
toward the river, thinking that she might have risen early
and gone to fetch water or to bathe.

When he reached the river he discovered that Ollokot,
as usual, was in the thick of things, and making smart
decisions. The only way down to the river from the tops
of the bluffs, without going a long way to the north or
south, was a steep ravine. Ollokot saw this in a glance,
and led two dozen warriors equipped with repeating
rifles from the battlefield at White Bird Canyon into this
ravine.

The yellowlegs up on the rimrock were firing down
into the camp indiscriminately. Dalton saw several dead
or dying women, and a young girl child with a big,
bloody hole in her chest. As he got to the river a warrior
was shot down directly in front of him. In his haste
Dalton had left the skin lodge without either the
Schofield or the Hawken. He scooped up the dead man's
repeating rifle and fired at the crest of the bluffs until the
gun was empty. Seven shots, and he thought that at least
one counted—a soldier pitched forward to cartwheel
down the sheer face of the bluff, bouncing once like a
limp rag doll before disappearing into the brush at the
base.

Throwing down the empty rifle, Dalton searched up
and down the river, looking for Light, oblivious to the hot
lead sizzling the air around him, calling out her name

until he was hoarse, his anxiety reaching fever pitch. And then he found her, huddled behind a log which lay half out of the water. He led her away from the river, shielding her with his own body.

The howitzer was still raining shells down upon the Nez Percé encampment. They found Toohoolzote, standing in the smoke and dust and ruin, a child's lifeless body in his arms, tears streaking his cheeks. Dalton persuaded him to put the dead child down and asked him to escort Light to safety beyond the howitzer's range. In this way he would also get the song singer out of immediate danger.

With Light taken care of, Dalton turned his full attention to the fight. Pausing at his skin lodge, he donned boots and gray tunic, scooped up the Schofield and the Hawken. The Nez Percé warriors who saw his gray coat were encouraged. They were accustomed to following it to victory. He ran back to the river, swam it, and started up the ravine, looking for Ollokot. He was not alone. Twenty warriors climbed with him. They reached Ollokot in time to join him in a daring charge out of a jumble of boulders which marked the head of the ravine, into the rear echelons of One Hand's force, throwing the yellowlegs into confusion. It was very much like what had happened at White Bird Canyon, and Dalton contemptuously realized that the bluecoats were slow to learn from their mistakes. Howard pulled his men back from the rim of the bluffs and formed a defensive square. His soldiers desperately dug shallow rifle pits with their bayonets. A few reckless warriors tried to charge into the square, but were driven back by the murderous fire of two Gatling guns.

Dalton led a dozen warriors around to the east of the soldiers, and almost captured the army's pack train, but it escaped into the square. For the remainder of the day

Indians and soldiers exchanged fire at such long range that it was largely ineffective. With the Hawken buffalo gun, Dalton managed to pick off several careless yellowlegs. The image of slaughtered Nez Percé women and children was seared into his mind, and he was satisfied with his work. Glad, too, that they had managed to pin Howard down, thereby giving Joseph time to get the rest of the tribe safely away.

The long and bloody day was drawing to a close when General Howard sent for Major Wettermark, who found his commander huddled down in the middle of the square, where a depression in the rocky ground provided some shelter from Indian gunfire. It occurred to Wettermark that he had not seen Howard on the front lines all day long, and he could not help but wonder how this man had ever earned a Medal of Honor.

Wettermark, on the other hand, had been in the thick of the fight. His gaunt face and uniform were covered with dust. There was blood on the uniform, as well. Not his own, though it struck others as little short of miraculous that the major, who had with cool courage and audacity exposed himself to enemy fire on a number of occasions to save the lives of wounded soldiers or to spur the men to stand firm, had not been so much as scratched. The blood on his uniform came from the wounds of other soldiers, men he had tried to help. He'd seen entirely too many men shot down this day, and as a consequence was not in the best humor as he stood to attention before Howard and saluted.

"Major," said One Hand, "I would say your estimates of enemy strength were grossly in error. I am told we are surrounded by at least four hundred warriors."

And that is exactly what he will put in his report, thought Wettermark.

"Nonsense," he replied curtly. "A hundred and fifty at most. But some of them have repeating rifles now. . . . "

Howard's eyes narrowed to slits. "This is unacceptable. We are completely boxed in. If we had not rescued the pack train, we would be running out of ammunition now."

Wettermark nodded. It was he who had led a dozen men in a desperate foray to save the beleaguered pack train. He sorely wanted to tell Howard that had he waited for orders to do so, the supplies would have been lost. But in spite of his foul mood he had better sense.

"The men are suffering from lack of water, General," he said.

"Good God," groaned Howard.

"There is a spring not a hundred yards south along the bluff." Wettermark could scarcely believe that he had to tell Howard the men were short on drinking water in the first place, or that Howard had not bothered to acquaint himself with the terrain, including the spring, in the second.

"No. We would do better to try to break out to the east."

"East? You mean retreat?" Wettermark was aghast. "General, may I suggest you get rid of your Nez Percé scouts?"

"What does that have to do with anything, Major?"

Wettermark's tone was acerbic. "You are poorly informed regarding what is occurring here today. This is not another Little Bighorn, although a few of your officers are beginning to panic because they think it might be. The Nez Percé scouts are not your allies. I believe that in general their sympathies lie with their nontreaty brethren. All they are interested in is your gold and your whiskey. If they are the ones who have told you we are facing four hundred warriors, then they flat out lied to you, and they know it. We do not need to retreat. We must attack. Ollokot and his bunch are just trying to keep us pinned down to give the encampment down below time to pack everything on travois and gather in the horse herd."

"You are suggesting we attack? Where?"

"All along the line. In every direction at once. And if you will lend me the howitzer and twenty good men, I'll capture the spring."

Howard thought it over as he listened to the sporadic shooting on all sides of the square. Wettermark's calculated mention of Custer's disaster at Little Bighorn last year did the trick, as the major had hoped it would. Howard was shaken by the ferocity of the Nez Percé attack, but concern for his own place in history stiffened his backbone.

He nodded. "Very well. You will have your howitzer and your twenty men. Take that spring at all costs, Major." He turned to one of his aides. "Inform all officers that they will attack the enemy in their front one half-hour from now. Tell them that if they are thinking about Little Bighorn, now is the time and the place to avenge our valiant comrades of the Seventh Cavalry, and restore some luster to the good name of the United States Army."

Wettermark turned and walked away, wondering bitterly why it was that firing shells into an unsuspecting village and killing innocent women and children did not tarnish the reputation of the United States Army. He supposed it was because the victims were red savages.

"Major Wettermark!"

He turned to find Zebulon Bigelow there, a mangled cigar in his teeth, one side of his face blackened with powder burn. The correspondent seemed utterly oblivious to the fact that a battle was going on, or to the possibility that a bullet could at any instant terminate his career. Actually, he looked very relaxed and sanguine, as though he were taking an evening constitutional along the sidewalk of some uptown Baltimore boulevard, rather than in the dust and din of a frontier fight.

"Mr. Bigelow, you had better get back to the pack train," advised Wettermark. "A man could get killed out here, and that's not your job."

Bigelow brushed aside this admonition with a gesture of careless disdain. Excitement danced across his chubby features. "I've seen him!" he exclaimed. "It's him! I've seen him with my own two eyes."

"Seen who?"

"The one they call the Gray Warrior."

"Where?"

"Over there." Bigelow pointed. "Lieutenant Connors was kind enough to loan me his fieldglasses. A splendid pair of Vollmers, I must say. I saw him quite clearly, among the rocks at the top of the draw, with the Indians. He was wearing his gray tunic. There was no mistaking him. His name is Dalton. He is the same man I last saw a dozen years ago at the train station in Columbus, Ohio. I guarantee it, Major."

"Then he must be the Confederate officer who killed those soldiers in Franklin," murmured Wettermark. "I'll be damned."

"Come on. I'll show you where he was just moments ago."

Wettermark shook his head. He had an odd, tingling feeling at the base of his spine. "No," he said softly. "Not yet."

"What?"

"I don't believe in coincidence, do you, Mr. Bigelow?"

"Well, I can't honestly say that I have given it much thought. . . . "

"I have. And I don't think it's a coincidence that Dalton and I are here. I chased him across half of this

country twelve years ago, and even then somehow I knew
I'd find him. He and I will meet when the time comes.
Right now I want you to get back to the pack train before
you get your fool head shot off. That's an order. So, if
you'll excuse me, I have an attack to lead."

20

The following day one of Howard's dispatch riders was ambushed and killed on his way to Fort Lapwei. Inside his case were found One Hand's first reports of the Battle of the Clearwater. The warriors who killed the dispatch rider did not know what the words on these papers signified, but, thinking they might be important, decided to take them to Joseph or Toohoolzote or Graycoat, any one of whom could decipher the report.

They found Graycoat first, at a place on the Clearwater, near Kamiah, where bullboats had been made and the Nez Percé were in the process of crossing to the east bank, on their way to Weippe Prairie. One Hand's counterattack had worked just as Major Wettermark had predicted it would. But once he had regained the rim of the bluff and the spring, One Hand had paused to regroup, allowing the Nez Percé to escape. When, finally, he did press the pursuit, five warriors led by the cunning Yellow Wolf delayed their crossing of the river for two hours. Five against five hundred—it was a feat which would be remembered for as long as there was one Nez Percé still alive.

Now Graycoat and Ollokot and twenty warriors were

acting as a rearguard while the river crossing was accomplished—the latter no easy task with so many women and children and belongings, not to mention the three thousand horses in the herd. Only Graycoat among them could read the dispatches, which he proceeded to do, translating them into Nez Percé. For the most part he no longer required the services of Toohoolzote to act as his guide through the intricacies of the Nez Percé tongue.

What they heard made Ollokot and the other warriors laugh out loud. One Hand was proclaiming a great victory. He was saying he had captured most of the Nez Percé horse herd, eighty lodges with many of the Indians' possessions, slain fifteen warriors in the battle, and captured forty more.

"None of this is true!" exclaimed Ollokot. "We left behind a few lame horses and some lodges because we knew the yellowlegs would waste time in looting them. Our scouts have told us that is exactly what they did. We lost only four warriors in the fight—Red Thunder and Going Across and two others. As for the ones he claims to have captured, they were Red Heart and a party of buffalo hunters, treaty Nez Percé returning to the reservation after a hunt. Graycoat, why does One Hand lie? A Nez Percé would never lie about his exploits in this way. It is shameful."

Dalton nodded. "He is afraid to tell the truth. Afraid he would appear incompetent."

"He is incompetent!" said Ollokot.

"No. He simply did not realize what great fighters the Nez Percé are. Now he knows. He will be ready next time."

The warriors brushed this warning aside. They had defeated the yellowlegs at White Bird Canyon. Though greatly outnumbered, they had fought them to a draw at Cottonwood House and the Clearwater. They did not have ears for Dalton's somber caveats. They laughed long and heartily at the lies One Hand had put in his report.

It was to be the last time Dalton ever heard a Nez Percé laugh.

They camped on the Weippe Prairie. With the river between them and One Hand the Nez Percé felt reasonably secure. Scouts were posted along the backtrail to keep an eye on the yellowlegs while others were sent ahead into the valley of the Kamiah, where a couple of hundred white settlers now lived. These settlers stood between the Nez Percé and the Lolo Trail. Would they take up their rifles against the Indians? If so, the Nez Percé would find themselves trapped between the yellowlegs and the *Shoyapee* civilians.

Dalton rode with the scouts into the Kamiah, and was relieved to find that the way to the Lolo Trail lay open. The settlers had abandoned their fields and cabins and moved to the towns or the fort or wherever they thought they would be better protected from the Indian menace.

He got back to the camp at Weippe Prairie in time for another council. He was beginning to tire of these meetings. In his opinion, if the Nez Percé spent less time talking and more time on the move they could very well be across the mountains by now.

The confidence which Dalton had witnessed among the warriors was not shared by the headmen or the women and children. The people were discouraged. At first Dalton was at a loss to know why. Then, when Joseph rose to speak to the council, he began to understand.

"For many days I have looked into my heart," said Joseph, "and now I know what it is we must do. I will say this only once. Then I will never speak of it again. We cannot run away from the *Shoyapee*. They are everywhere. We will not be safe even in the land of the Crow. One

Hand will follow us there. We have embarrassed him in the eyes of his own people, and he will not rest until he has caught us. Many of our own people are saddened, because they realize that once we cross the mountains we will bid farewell forever to our land, where the bones of our forefathers lie. Once I too said we should run away. But now I see that it would be futile."

"So what do you suggest we do?" asked old Looking Glass, headman of the Asotin band.

"We must go into the mountains and there make our stand."

"But we would all be killed!"

Joseph's sad eyes searched the circle of faces illumined by the council fire, and came to rest on Dalton.

"Once my only concern was for the children. I was afraid the white man would try to make our children ashamed of their heritage. But what would our children say if we ran away and abandoned our land to the *Shoyapee*? Would they not be ashamed? They would hang their heads. No, we must surrender and go meekly to the reservation, or stand and fight. Otherwise the yellowlegs will hunt us down and catch us and drag us back in chains, and the once proud Nez Percé will be no more. Ask Graycoat. He has fought the yellowlegs longer than any of us. Once he tried to run away."

Dalton stood up. "*Tukug*, Joseph. You are right. It is as you say."

Looking Glass shot to his feet with an agility astonishing in one so old.

"No! Joseph is not right. We must go to the Crow country. One Hand will leave us alone once we are across the mountains. The war will be over. We will still be free. We must listen no longer to Joseph. He means well. He truly speaks his heart. But his heart is wrong. Once he told us to trust the white man, and this we did. The white man has betrayed that trust. He has stolen our horses, raped our women, burned our villages, infected our children with his diseases. And now look at us! This is what has come from trusting the white man. Now Joseph changes his mind and says it is better to die on our land than to leave it. He says we must fight. But where was Joseph in the fight at the White Bird? Where was he in the fight on the Clearwater? No. The way is clear. We can escape. We must cross the mountains. I know that country to the east. I know the people there. Even the whites there will be friendly. We will be able to live in peace."

Dalton shook his head. But the council was inclined to agree with Looking Glass. That Joseph had been conspicuously absent from the fighting of the past two weeks had done grave damage to his credibility. Dalton did not think this was fair. The man had to have great courage, to have done all that he had done in standing up to the whites and opposing the treaties with which they had robbed the Nez Percé of their land. But the warriors could not see this. All they saw was Joseph staying behind with the women and children when the shooting started. Dalton believed it was because Joseph adamantly refused to take the life of another human being. He never had, and even locked in a desperate struggle for survival he would not. But that didn't make him a coward. Far from it.

Now here was Joseph urging his people to stand and fight. Coming from him this just didn't strike the warriors as credible. Dalton really couldn't blame them for being skeptical. You could not ask a man to stand and die for a cause if you did not appear to be willing to do the same.

That very night, while the council was still in progress, a scout arrived in the camp with the unwelcome news that One Hand was on the move, crossing the Clearwater, and hot on their trail.

The next morning the travois were loaded, the horse herd gathered, and the Nez Percé proceeded across the valley of the Kamiah to the Lolo Trail.

The Lolo Trail was the only way across the Bitterroots from the Kamiah Valley. It proved to be a very difficult crossing. The trail was steep and winding, and obstructed by vast deadfalls. To make matters worse, a cold and drenching rain began to fall, and continued unabated for days. This deluge triggered avalanches, and made the footing treacherous. The path of the fleeing Nez Percé was strewn with the carcasses of dead horses which had broken their legs and been put to death. Dozens of ponies and several old people perished. Toohoolzote admitted to Dalton that he wondered if Hunyewat, the god of the Nez Percé, had decided to punish his people for abandoning their homeland to the whites. With each passing day the Nez Percé grew increasingly discouraged.

General Howard was determined to pursue his Indian prey across the mountains, but a small band of warriors led by Rainbow ambushed the column as it entered the Bitterroots. They were so strongly entrenched among some boulders which commanded the trail that Howard could not dislodge them. One Hand became discouraged, too. He informed the War Department that the non-treaties were no longer in his Department of the Columbia, and he questioned his authority to continue after them. The War Department ordered him to press on after the Nez Percé. Howard took a fortnight to reorganize and resupply. Wettermark concluded that Howard had decided in his own mind to give Joseph and the renegades every opportunity to escape. Wettermark didn't think this was because Howard was sympathetic; rather, he had been outwitted and outfought by the Indians at every turn, and once burned made twice shy.

At least it did not seem as though Howard had much desire to be the one who captured the renegades. That seemed odd at first glance, for a man so consumed by the advancement of his own career. Bigelow told Wettermark he thought it was because the general had heard that the big eastern newspapers were beginning to say that American public opinion was swinging to the side of the Indians. "It may be," said the canny correspondent, "that the man who finally brings Joseph down won't be the hero of the piece at all. In fact, he could very well turn out to be the villain. I think General Howard realizes this."

It was the end of July before Howard started up the Lolo Trail, with seven hundred men, including Narrow Eyes Chapman and the Nez Percé scouts. By then the nontreaties were long gone, and Rainbow had pulled back. Details of axe-wielding troopers cut the way through the deadfalls. The Nez Percé were well ahead of the yellowlegs now, descending the eastern flank of the Bitterroots, with the high plains of the Crow country beckoning to them.

But the War Department had sent a detachment of regulars commanded by Captain Charles Rawn to block the eastern mouth of the trail, thereby bottling up the Indians. Rawn was joined by civilian volunteers from the Bitterroot Valley. A log barricade was erected, and Rawn's men were prepared for an all-out attack. Instead, the Nez Percé sent emissaries to hold a series of lengthy councils with Rawn, who, believing the Indians to be sincere in their talk of surrender, had visions of national fame as the man who had nabbed Chief Joseph. But Rawn never even laid eyes on Joseph, whose plan it was to keep Rawn occupied while the main body of Indians climbed to higher ground and circled around the barricade. Some of the warriors wanted to fight, but most of the people were so tired and hungry that they were quite satisfied

with the subterfuge. By the time Rawn found out he had
been fooled, the Indians were in the valley, and his command was entirely too small to attack them out in the open.

By the time Howard reached the Bitterroot Valley, the
Nez Percé were across the next range of mountains and in
the valley of the Big Hole. Here Looking Glass found
some white traders who knew him and were willing to
sell the Indians some supplies. Looking Glass assured the
people they could pause and rest for a while in this place.
He was well acquainted with Montana, and weren't the
traders proof that many of the whites here were friendly?
Besides, where was One Hand? He had given up,
declared Looking Glass. There was no need to worry.

Dalton didn't think it was a good idea to stop. Neither
did Joseph. But the people were in no mood to listen to
either one of them. They were exhausted, and wanted to
believe Looking Glass, so they made camp at a place called
Its-koom-tse-le-lick, Place of the Ground Squirrels.

Early the next morning, an hour prior to dawn,
Toohoolzote found Dalton saddling the mouse-colored
mustang. Light was already mounted. Their lodgepoles
and scant belongings were strapped to a travois tied to
Light's horse.

"Where are you going, Graycoat?" asked the song
singer, shocked.

"We're leaving."

"But why?"

"This is foolish, Toohoolzote, camping here in this valley. I promise you, the soldiers are coming. They haven't
given up. Yet you haven't sent out any scouts, and many
of your young warriors are drunk on rotgut bought from
the traders."

"Where will you go?"

"Canada," said Dalton.

Toohoolzote nodded sadly. "Yes, I think it is time for

you to go your own way. I, too, have a bad feeling. I am glad you and Light are going, before it is too late."

Dalton shook the Indian's hand. "I'm just tired of being at war, old friend."

Toohoolzote smiled. "I am glad. I will sing a good song for you. The Coyote will listen, and I think he will grant you peace and happiness for the rest of your life."

Dalton climbed into the saddle, took one last look at the Nez Percé who had been his truest friend, and rode away, Light beside him. There were a few early risers in the village, and they watched him go in silence. Dalton began to have second thoughts about leaving. He felt as though he were deserting these people. But one look at Light renewed his resolve. There was nothing he could do for the Nez Percé now. They were doomed. They had no future. He did. He had a reason to live.

A mile from the village Dalton suddenly checked his horse sharply. Light started to ask him what was wrong, but his sharp gesture silenced her. Then she heard what he was hearing—the unmistakable sound of many horses. It was very faint, but seemed to be coming from the other side of the tree-cloaked ridge which loomed above the grassy meadow which they had been crossing.

Dalton abruptly angled his horse up the slope of the ridge. Light followed. Near the crest he dismounted, and motioned for her to do likewise. They led their horses the rest of the way. At the top they could look down through the pines and see the valley below. It was choked with soldiers. Dalton figured there had to be at least two hundred of them.

And they were heading straight for the village of the Nez Percé.

21

"I've got to go back, Light."

"No," she cried softly, clutching at his arm. "You will surely die."

"I've got to warn them. They don't have any scouts . . . "

"You will die," she said. "I feel it."

"I'm going. Stay here. Promise that you will wait for me right here, Light."

She looked around. The soughing of the wind in the tops of the pines, a lonely and mournful sound, seemed to echo the sorrow in her heart.

"I will wait," she said. "If you do not come back, this is where I will die."

"Don't be silly, Light. I'll be back."

Climbing back into the saddle, Dalton wheeled the mustang around and descended the ridge. At the bottom of the slope he kicked his horse into a stretched-out run.

It was the longest mile he had ever traveled. But when he emerged from a line of trees and saw the Nez Percé horse herd, and beyond the herd the peaceful village, he was relieved. He'd beaten the soldiers. He'd made it in time.

The first person he saw was an old man, bundled up in a blanket against the dawn chill, smoking a pipe as he sat on a log and watched the horses graze in the tall grass. His own pony stood behind him, tethered to the log. As Dalton checked the gray, the old man looked up at him with expressionless eyes.

"There are soldiers coming, father," said Dalton, in the Nez Percé tongue. "Return to the village."

The old man nodded gravely. Dalton rode on, scattering the ponies. He had gone less than a hundred yards when the crack of a rifle made him jump. Then several more rifles spoke. He checked the horse again and looked back—to see the old man lying dead, draped across the log, and beyond, a line of blue-clad soldiers charging out of the woods. A bullet whined past Dalton's ear. Bent low, he kicked the mustang into a gallop.

The old man had been unarmed. Dalton was furious—at the soldiers, for killing a harmless old man, and at the Nez Percé, too, for putting the old one out there in harm's way in the first place.

Many of the horses in the cavallard were running through the camp, and only added to the confusion. The soldiers were riding in behind them, and immediately the battle became a hand-to-hand struggle.

A cavalryman came galloping around a skin lodge so suddenly that Dalton's horse collided with his, an impact so severe and unexpected that both men and both horses went down. Dalton rolled and came up with the Schofield in one hand and the Hawken still gripped in the other. The soldier was quick to his feet as well. They fired simultaneously, less than ten paces apart. Dalton's bullet caught the man in the throat. Somehow the soldier missed. Dalton could scarcely believe it, at this range.

In a glance he saw that his mustang had broken a foreleg. Without hesitation, but with considerable remorse, he put a bullet in the animal's brain pan, and the mustang ceased to writhe in agony.

For a moment Dalton stood there as a hurricane of violence swirled around him. On every hand there was dust and death and powdersmoke, screams and shouts and gunfire. Some of the soldiers were mounted. Others were afoot, bulling their way into skin lodges with guns blazing, spraying hot lead, killing anything that moved. Dalton saw an old Nez Percé who had spread his blanket in front of his lodge and settled down cross-legged to smoke his pipe and wait stoically for death. The yellowlegs obliged him, and his body was riddled with bullets. Dalton saw, too, a naked woman running, a scream of terror on her lips, pursued by a soldier who plunged a bayonet into her back between the shoulder blades. The woman fell, writhing, and begged for mercy. The soldier smashed her face into a bloody pulp with the stock of his rifle—just before falling across her with the point of a lance jutting from his chest.

Feeling the ground tremble beneath his feet, Dalton whirled to see a mounted soldier bearing down on him with pistol blazing. A bullet smashed into Dalton's arm, staggering him, but he managed to trigger the primed and loaded Hawken, and the soldier's horse screamed and died in midstride. The trooper was hurled from the saddle and broke his neck in the fall.

Arm numb and practically useless, Dalton discarded the empty Hawken and kept moving. He relied on the Schofield now, and the revolver spoke five more times in the next minute. There were plenty of targets, as he worked his way towards the center of the came, where Joseph's lodge stood. The dead and dying were strewn everywhere. The smoke and dust was so thick he could hardly see fifty feet in front of him.

What he did see horrified him. A mounted soldier riding down a young boy; the horse's hooves turned the screaming youth into a bleeding clump of mangled human clay. With an animal snarl on his lips, Dalton broke into a run. But Toohoolzote reached the soldier first. The song singer appeared out of nowhere and launched himself at the soldier, dragging him from his saddle. The peace-loving Toohoolzote was like a madman. He had a horse soldier's pistol, and he shoved the barrel into the yellowleg's mouth and pulled the trigger. Two bluecoats charged out of the smoke at him. Toohoolzote gunned one of them down, but the second one impaled the song singer on his bayonet. Dalton's hoarse yell was drowned out by the din of battle. The Schofield was empty, and he was too far away to save his friend. Yet even as he fell Toohoolzote shot his killer in the face.

When Dalton reached him, Toohoolzote was holding up a handful of dirt and watching it as it trickled through his fingers. Seeing Dalton, the song singer managed a bloody smile.

"I wish this was Nez Percé land," he said, and then he died.

Dalton heard Joseph's voice. There, in the center of the camp, the Wallowa headman stood in front of his skin lodge, with two dozen warriors formed in a circle around him. Two small children clung to Joseph. The warriors were all armed with repeating rifles, and the ground in front of them was carpeted with blue-clad bodies. Joseph stood tall, wrapped in his King George blanket, talking calmly to the warriors. "We will hold here. Shoot low. Do not waste your ammunition." Inspired by his calm courage, more and more Indians were flocking to him. "We are holding here," he called out to his people. "Bring the women and children to me." Soon there were fifty warriors in the circle, with many women and children inside of it. Dalton stripped a repeater and ammunition pouch from a dead cavalryman and joined them.

The soldiers made three concerted assaults on the circle. Each one was thrown back. Then, suddenly, it was over. The yellowlegs were pulling back.

Dalton learned from a wounded officer, a lieutenant, that they were elements of the Seventh Infantry, supported by a company of cavalry and commanded by Colonel John Gibbon. General William Tecumseh Sherman, commander in chief of the forces engaged in the Nez Percé War, had dispatched Gibbon to the Big Hole Valley to find the Indians. Gibbon himself had been seriously injured in the fight, and a number of officers were slain, which threw the troops into disarray. But there were other units converging from all directions. Six companies of the Seventh Cavalry to the east, five companies of the Fifth Cavalry to the south, and, of course, Howard's command crossing the mountains to the west.

The camp was a scene of heart-rending anguish. Twenty warriors had fallen, including the legendary Rainbow, whose death had inspired his friend Five Wounds to launch a suicidal one-man attack against a squadron of horse soldiers. Five Wounds had long ago told his good friend that they would die on the same day. Worst of all, though, were the casualties among the women and children. More than sixty of them had been brutally cut down by the rampaging soldiers.

The yellowlegs had been beaten back once again—but this time Dalton witnessed no exultation among the Nez Percé. The Indians were whipped. He could see it in their eyes. They had won every battle, but lost the war. Now they knew old Looking Glass had been wrong. They were not safe in Crow country. The soldiers would never stop chasing them. With Looking Glass discredited, the people turned to Joseph. He was the one who had rallied them in the battle of Big Hole Valley.

"It is too late to make a stand in the mountains," he told Ollokot and Yellow Wolf. "The Lolo Trail belongs to One Hand now."

"Where will we go?" asked Ollokot. "What do we do now, brother?"

"Perhaps we should surrender," muttered Yellow Wolf.

These words surprised Dalton. Yellow Wolf had been rabid in his hatred of the whites. He had always been the one to speak for fighting to the death. But seeing the corpses of so many women and children discouraged him. He was not afraid for himself, but rather for his people.

"No," replied Joseph sternly. "Not yet. We will go north. Perhaps we can reach Canada. Sitting Bull of the Sioux lives there now, safe from the yellowlegs."

"I do not think we will make it to Canada," admitted Ollokot.

Joseph said nothing. But it was written all over his face—he didn't think so either.

"Will you come with us, Graycoat?" asked Yellow Wolf.

The answer was bitter on Dalton's tongue, and he was hesitant to speak. Joseph came to his rescue.

"No. Graycoat must leave us now. He has fought bravely with us many times. The least we can do is let him go his own way and bid him well. He should not have to share what the future holds in store for the Nez Percé. He has his own future. The soldiers would execute him if they caught him. I do not want to see that happen."

Yellow Wolf and Ollokot bid Dalton good-bye and walked away. Joseph was the last to shake his hand. The Wallowa headman's grip was firm.

"*Taz alago*, Graycoat."

"It is almost over, Joseph."

"I know. But I will not hand them a victory. They will have to earn it."

"Your children will be proud."

With that Dalton turned away. Mounted on a roan horse bearing a U.S. brand, he left the Nez Percé Indians for the last time.

A little while later he was back on the wooded ridge where he had parted with Light. She was waiting for him, and wept silent tears of joy to see her man alive. She wanted to tend to the wound in his arm, but he shook his head. There wasn't time. The bullet had gone clean through. And this country was crawling with soldiers.

They turned their horses north.

Howard arrived at the scene of the Battle of Big Hole Valley a day after the fight. The Nez Percé were gone. They had left their dead behind, something they would not have done except for the fact that Gibbon's veteran soldiers had rallied during the night and kept the pressure on. It was all Joseph could do to take the wounded and slip away under the cover of darkness. When dawn broke the soldiers learned that their prey had slipped through their clutches, leaving only a handful of warriors led by Ollokot to discourage pursuit.

When Howard learned that thirty soldiers had been killed, and forty wounded, and still the Indians had escaped, despite the fact that Gibbon had enjoyed the advantage of surprise, he was furious.

"We will press on immediately," he told his subordinates. "I know the men are weary. But there is no help for it. Those savages must be stopped."

"Savages?" Wettermark had spent an hour wandering in a kind of horrified daze through the Nez Percé camp. Now something inside him snapped. "Did you say 'savages,' General? What do you call the men who killed those women and children out there? What do you call the bastard who ground an infant's head beneath the heel of his boot? What do you call the man who cut the breasts off a young Indian woman, whose body is lying not a hundred yards from this very spot? What our soldiers did here yesterday turns my stomach. It makes me ashamed to wear this uniform."

Howard was aghast. He glanced at the other officers, and could tell by the expressions on their faces that Wettermark's words had affected them. For some reason he could not comprehend this enraged him.

"That's enough, Major!" he snapped. "The rest of you are dismissed."

When the others were out of earshot Howard turned on Wettermark. "By God, Major, from now on you had better curb your tongue, or I'll bust you down to private."

The threat did not faze Wettermark. "You once told me you wanted candid assessments. Well, General, here's one for you to chew on. When this is all over, public sentiment will have turned against you. Joseph will be the hero, and rightly so, I might add."

"I can see you will be of no further use to me, Major," rasped Howard icily, his face almost as red as his beard. "Therefore, I am giving you a special mission. Reports from some of Colonel Gibbon's officers indicate that the white man the Indians call Graycoat has left Joseph and gone north. Clearly he is trying to save his neck and escape to Canada. I want you to capture him, Major. He is a traitor to his country, and he must be brought to justice. Bring him back. And do not fail."

"Yes, sir. May I request that Mr. Bigelow accompany me?"

"By all means. I'm sick and tired of having that troublemaker underfoot. You will be assigned a detail of ten men. Lieutenant Connors will go with you. You will leave immediately."

Wettermark was happy to oblige. His conscience would not let him linger in Big Hole Valley.

The stage was set for the final, tragic act in the saga of the Nez Percé and their flight to freedom.

Many of the wounded from the Battle of the Big Hole Valley perished as Joseph led his people north in a desperate race for the Canadian border. Although Joseph tried to prevent it, angry young warriors raided farms and ranches along the way, and several civilians were killed. Ollokot managed to slow the pursuit down by leading a raiding party to scatter One Hand's mule herd.

As the Nez Percé fled through Yellowstone country, a group of nine tourists were taken hostage. Once the Indians were across the Absaroka range the hostages were released unharmed. Their adventures were plastered all over the front pages of eastern newspapers within the week. There was growing sympathy for the plight of Joseph and his people as a result, but it was dampened by reports of the farmers and ranchers who had fallen victim to the young warriors.

Somehow Joseph slipped through the army's grasp on the Yellowstone River, but the respite was brief. While Colonel Nelson Miles struck out from Fort Keogh to place himself across the path of the Indians, Colonel Samuel Sturgis led four hundred Seventh Cavalry troopers in hot pursuit, leaving Howard and his weary ranks of infantry behind. Sturgis caught the Nez Percé at Canyon Creek. Once again the Indians managed to escape, only to find themselves harassed by Bannock and Crow warriors who had served as scouts for Sturgis.

More disillusioned than ever, the Nez Percé finally reached the Missouri River. September was drawing to a close. Arctic winds and whipping snows made of every mile an ordeal. They took much-needed food from a steamboat freight depot and crossed the Bear Paw Mountains. Realizing his people were too exhausted to go on without some rest, Joseph made camp on Snake Creek, a tributary of the Milk River. Here they were attacked by Miles, who, in addition to four hundred regulars, had a company of Sioux and Cheyenne scouts, a Hotchkiss gun, and a Napoleon cannon. Though the Nez Percé once again prevailed against superior numbers in fierce hand-to-hand fighting, Miles did manage to make off with their horses. Afoot, the Nez Percé could only dig in and make a stand. They had lost many warriors in the last fight, including the dauntless and irreplaceable Ollokot. Surrounded by the yellowlegs, they held out for five days, despite a heavy snow and bitter cold, no food, and precious little ammunition.

Accompanied by a small detachment, two friendly Nez Percé scouts, and the Indian-hater called Narrow Eyes Chapman, Howard arrived at Snake Creek early on the fifth day of the siege. The general sent his two scouts in to negotiate a surrender. Joseph called a final council. He argued for surrender, in order to spare his people further suffering. A few of the warriors were adamantly opposed, and managed to slip through the enemy's lines. Most of these reached Canada safely. But the majority of Nez Percé gave up that afternoon. Joseph offered his rifle to One Hand.

"I am weary of war," he said. "My brother, Ollokot, is dead. The little children are freezing. We have no blankets, and no food. My heart is sick with anguish for the suffering of my people. Colonel Miles has said we may return to our land if we surrender. Is this what you say, One Hand?"

"I'll make sure of it," lied Howard.

"Then from where the sun now stands I will fight no more forever."

Their epic flight was over. Seven hundred and fifty Nez Percé had covered fifteen hundred miles, pursued by over two thousand troops, fought four major battles and dozens of skirmishes, during a period of three months. Now, eighty-seven men and three hundred women and children were shipped to a pestilence-ridden camp near Fort Leavenworth, Kansas, and held as prisoners of war, in spite of the violent protests of Colonel Nelson Miles. That winter more than twenty perished from lack of food and medicine. The following summer, the survivors were transferred to their new home, the barren northeast corner of the Indian Territory.

Thanks to shortcuts revealed to him by Bannock scouts, Wettermark caught up with Dalton and Light on the Canadian border.

While six troopers stayed on Dalton's tail, Wettermark—accompanied by Lieutenant Connors, four cavalrymen, and Zebulon Bigelow—allowed the pair of Bannocks to guide him to a spot overlooking a notch through which their prey would have to pass. By dawn they were in position on a high, grassy hill giving them a clear view of the notch. After all, they could do nothing but wait.

It was a gray and blustery October day. While Connors kept watch with his prized Vollmer binoculars, Wettermark stretched out on the damp ground, wrapped in his blanket, and pulled his campaign hat down over his face. He pretended to be asleep, because he had a lot of thinking to do and did not want to be disturbed. Bigelow chewed on a cigar and tried to write, though the cold wind that swept the hilltop threatened to carry away his paper, and the occasional splattering raindrop smeared his ink. The two Bannocks went off a little ways and sat on their heels and watched, waiting with that unflappable patience which Wettermark had come to expect from Indians.

"Here they come," said Connors.

The troopers grabbed their rifles and knelt in a line along the crest of the hill, spaced well apart. Connors had made it a point to bring along the best shots in the detail. The range would be a couple hundred yards, no hill for a stepper. The only thing that made it the least bit interesting was the wind, but Connors had faith in his sharpshooters.

With a sigh, Wettermark rose, planted the campaign hat firmly on his head, and joined Connors. Bigelow was right behind him.

Down below, two riders had emerged from the jumble of rocks which marked the notch. They rode single file. There was no mistaking the tunic of butternut-gray worn by the rider in front.

"What about the squaw, Lieutenant?" drawled one of the troopers.

"She is a renegade. Shoot her."

"Seems like a waste," said the trooper, and spat a stream of yellowish-brown tobacco juice.

"Damn you," muttered Wettermark.

Connors and the troopers looked sharply at him. Wettermark had his revolver out of its flap holster. He held the gun down by his side.

"No point in trying to take him alive," said Connors. "He won't give up without a fight. Why risk the lives of my men . . . "

"The first man who shoots gets a bullet in the brain," said Wettermark.

"What?" Connors was sure he hadn't heard right.

"Let them pass."

"Are you insane?" exclaimed Connors. "They'll escape. That's Canada over the next rise, Major."

"Good."

Connors's cheeks were mottled with anger. "What the hell are you doing, Major Wettermark?"

"Making amends, Lieutenant. Making amends."

Connors didn't understand that, and didn't care. "You'll stand before a court-martial for this. I'll see to it."

"No, you won't," said Bigelow mildly. There was steel

lurking behind his cherubic smile. "You won't say a word about this. None of you will. If you do, I'll see to it that your names are the most reviled in the history of the republic. And I can do it, too. The pen, you know, is mightier than the sword."

A minute dragged by. Nobody moved or spoke. The howling wind was the only sound. Then another minute came and went. And another. Connors stared at the gun in Wettermark's hand.

"Well," drawled the trooper who had asked about shooting Turns from the Light, "it don't much matter now. They're out of range."

Infuriated, Connors turned on his heel and stalked away. Wettermark wearily holstered his revolver. With a nod of thanks to Bigelow, he went to his horse, came back carrying a sword in a scabbard.

"You never told me, Ben, where you got that," said Bigelow.

"Maybe I will someday."

Wettermark drew the sword, drove the blade into the ground, and dropped the scabbard beside it. With one last look at the two riders below, he turned away, snapping a curt order to the troopers to mount up.

Bigelow tarried on the hilltop, gnashing the short six between his teeth, watching until Dalton and Light were mere specks on the rim of the hill to the north. Then they were gone, and the correspondent grinned, thinking that maybe there was after all a little justice left in this old world.

AN ORDINARY MAN
by J. R. McFarland

A drifting lawman with a knack for killing, MacLane was a lonely man—until an odd twist changed his fate. Only then did he have the chance to change the course of his life and become an ordinary man with an extraordinary message to deliver.

GRAY WARRIOR
by Hank Edwards

Jack Dalton was a rebel who would never surrender—even if it killed him. But the love of a beautiful woman brings changes all the killing in the world could not. In a savage wilderness of bullets and blood, Dalton finds something bigger and better than himself, something worth living for.